Beyond
Therapy

by
Christopher Durang

SAMUEL FRENCH, INC.

45 WEST 25TH STREET   NEW YORK 10010
7623 SUNSET BOULEVARD HOLLYWOOD 90046
LONDON   TORONTO

BROOKS ATKINSON THEATRE

UNDER THE DIRECTION OF THE MESSRS. NEDERLANDER

WARNER THEATRE PRODUCTIONS / CLAIRE NICHTERN
FDM PRODUCTIONS / FRANCOIS de MENIL and HARRIS MASLANSKY
present

JOHN   DIANNE
LITHGOW   WIEST

in

BEYOND THERAPY

a new comedy by
CHRISTOPHER DURANG

with
PETER MICHAEL GOETZ

JACK GILPIN   DAVID PIERCE

and
KATE McGREGOR-STEWART

Settings by	Costumes by	Lighting by
ANDREW JACKNESS	**JENNIFER VON MAYRHAUSER**	**PAUL GALLO**

Music Coordinator **JACK FELDMAN**

Directed by
JOHN MADDEN

COMMISSIONED AND ORIGINALLY PRODUCED BY THE PHOENIX THEATRE

T. EDWARD HAMBLETON	**STEVEN ROBMAN**
Managing Director	Artistic Director

The Producers and Theatre Management are Members of the League of New York Theatres and Producers, Inc.
The Producers wish to express their appreciation to the Theatre Development Fund for its support of the production.

CAST

(*in order of appearance*)

Bruce .... JOHN LITHGOW

Prudence .... DIANNE WIEST

Stuart ... . PETER MICHAEL GOETZ

Charlotte .... KATE McGREGOR-STEWART

Bob .... JACK GILPIN

Andrew .... DAVID PIERCE

STANDBYS

Standbys never substitute for listed players unless a specific announcement
is made at the time of the performance.

For Bruce and Stuart — James Eckhouse.

BEYOND THERAPY was previously presented by the Phoenix Theatre in New York City on January 1, 1981. The production was directed by Jerry Zaks; scenery by Karen Schultz; costumes by Jennifer von Mayrhauser; lighting by Richard Nelson; sound by David Rapkin. The cast was as follow:

BRUCE ....Stephen Collins
PRUDENCE ....Sigourney Weaver
Dr. STUART FRAMINGHAM ....Jim Borelli
MRS. CHARLOTTE WALLACE ......
                          Kate McGregor-Stewart
BOB ....Jack Gilpin
ANDREW ....Conan McCarty
PAUL* ....Nick Stannard

*The character of Paul, a former suitor of Prudence's, appeared in the final scene of the play at the Phoenix. This scene was changed for the Broadway version, and the character was written out.

CAST
(in order of appearance)

BRUCE ....John Lithgow
PRUDENCE ....Dianne Wiest
STUART ....Peter Michael Goetz
CHARLOTTE ....Kate McGregor-Stewart
BOB ....Jack Gilpin
ANDREW ....David Pierce

SETTINGS BY Andrew Jackness
COSTUMES BY Jennifer Von Mayrhauser
LIGHTING BY Paul Gallo
PRODUCTION STAGE MANAGER:
   Craig Jacobs
MUSIC COORDINATOR: Jack Feldman
DIRECTED BY John Madden
PRODUCED BY Warner Theatre Productions
   (Claire Nichtern) and FDM/Productions
   (Francois de Menil and Harris Maslansky)

SYNOPSIS OF SCENES
ACT I

   Scene 1: A Restaurant
   Scene 2: Dr. Stuart Framingham's Office
   Scene 3: The Office of Charlotte Wallace
   Scene 4: The Restaurant Again
   Scene 5: Dr. Framingham's Office
   Scene 6: Bruce's Apartment

INTERMISSION
ACT II

   Scene 1: Mrs. Wallace's Office
   Scene 2: The Restaurant Again
   Scene 3: The Restaurant Still

BEYOND THERAPY

ACT I

Scene 1

A restaurant. BRUCE *is seated, looking at his watch.*
HE *is 30-34, fairly pleasant looking, probably wear-*
ing a blazer with an open shirt. Enter PRUDENCE,
29-32, attractive, semi-dressed up in a dress or
nice skirt and blouse. After hesitating a moment,
SHE *crosses to* BRUCE.

PRUDENCE. Hello.

BRUCE. Hello.

PRUDENCE. *(Perhaps referring to a newspaper in*
her hand—The New York Review of Books?) Are you
the white male, 30 to 35, 6'2", blue eyes, who's into
rock music, movies, jogging and quiet evenings at
home?

BRUCE. Yes, I am. *(Stands)*

PRUDENCE. Hi, I'm Prudence.

BRUCE. I'm Bruce.

PRUDENCE. Nice to meet you.

BRUCE. Won't you sit down?

PRUDENCE. Thank you. *(Sits)* As I said in my letter,
I've never answered one of these ads before.

BRUCE. Me neither. I mean, I haven't put one in
before.

7

PRUDENCE. But this time I figured, why not?

BRUCE. Right. Me too. (*Pause*) I hope I'm not too macho for you.

PRUDENCE. No. So far you seem wonderful.

BRUCE. You have lovely breasts. That's the first thing I notice in a woman.

PRUDENCE. Thank you.

BRUCE. You have beautiful contact lenses.

PRUDENCE. Thank you. I like the timbre of your voice. Soft but firm.

BRUCE. Thanks. I like *your* voice.

PRUDENCE. Thank you. I love the smell of Brut you're wearing.

BRUCE. Thank you. My male lover Bob gave it to me.

PRUDENCE. What?

BRUCE. You remind me of him in a certain light.

PRUDENCE. What?

BRUCE. I swing both ways actually. Do you?

PRUDENCE. (*Rattled, serious*) I don't know. I always insist on the lights being out.

(*Pause*)

BRUCE. I'm afraid I've upset you now.

PRUDENCE. No, it's nothing really. It's just that I hate gay people.

BRUCE. I'm not gay. I'm bisexual. There's a difference.

PRUDENCE. I don't really know any bisexuals.

BRUCE. Children are all innately bisexual, you know. If you took a child to Plato's Retreat, he'd be attracted to both sexes.

PRUDENCE. I should imagine he'd be terrified.

BRUCE. Well, he might be, of course. I've never taken a child to Plato's Retreat.

PRUDENCE. I don't think they let you.

BRUCE. I don't really know any children. (*Pause*) You have wonderful eyes. They're so deep.

PRUDENCE. Thank you.

BRUCE. I feel like I want to take care of you.

PRUDENCE. (*Liking this tack better*) I would like that. My favorite song is "Someone to Watch over Me."

BRUCE. (*Sings softly*) "There a somebody I'm longing duh duh..."

PRUDENCE. Yes. Thank you.

BRUCE. In some ways you're like a little girl. And in some ways you're like a woman.

PRUDENCE. How am I like a woman?

BRUCE. (*Searching, romantically*) You...dress like a woman. You wear eye shadow like a woman.

PRUDENCE. You're like a man. You're tall, you have to shave. I feel you could protect me.

BRUCE. I'm deeply emotional, I like to cry.

PRUDENCE. Oh I wouldn't like that.

BRUCE. But I *like* to cry.

PRUDENCE. I don't think men should cry unless something falls on them.

BRUCE. That's a kind of sexism. Men have been programmed not to show feeling.

PRUDENCE. Don't talk to me about sexism. You're the one who talked about my breasts the minute I sat down.

BRUCE. I feel like I'm going to cry now.

PRUDENCE. Why do you want to cry?

BRUCE. I feel you don't like me enough. I think you're making eyes at the waiter.

PRUDENCE. I haven't even seen the waiter.

(BRUCE *cries*)

PRUDENCE. (*Continued*) *Please*, don't cry, please.

BRUCE. (*Stops crying after a bit*) I feel better after that. You have a lovely mouth.

PRUDENCE. Thank you.

BRUCE. I can tell you're very sensitive. I want you to have my children.

PRUDENCE. Thank you.

BRUCE. Do you feel ready to make a commitment?

PRUDENCE. I feel I need to get to know you better.

BRUCE. I feel we agree on all the issues. I feel that you like rock music, movies, jogging, and quiet evenings at home. I think you hate shallowness. I bet you never read "People" magazine.

PRUDENCE. I do read it. I write for it.

BRUCE. I write for it too. Free lance actually. I send in letters. They printed one of them.

PRUDENCE. Oh, what was it about?

BRUCE. I wanted to see Gary Gilmore executed on television.

PRUDENCE. Oh, yes, I remember that one.

BRUCE. Did you identify with Jill Clayburgh in "An Unmarried Woman"?

PRUDENCE. Uh, yes, I did.

BRUCE. Me too! We agree on everything. I want to cry again.

PRUDENCE. I don't like men to cry. I want them to be strong.

BRUCE. You'd quite like Bob then.

PRUDENCE. Who?

BRUCE. You know.

PRUDENCE. Oh.

BRUCE. I feel I'm irritating you.

PRUDENCE. No. It's just that it's hard to get to know someone. And the waiter never comes, and I'd like to order.

BRUCE. Let's start all over again. Hello. My name is Bruce.

PRUDENCE. Hello.

BRUCE. Prudence. That's a lovely name.

PRUDENCE. Thank you.

BRUCE. That's a lovely dress.

PRUDENCE. Thank you. I like your necklace. It goes nicely with your chest hair.

BRUCE. Thank you. I like your nail polish.

PRUDENCE. I have it on my toes too.

BRUCE. Let me see.

(SHE *takes shoe off, puts foot on the table*)

BRUCE. (*Continued*) I think it's wonderful you feel free enough with me to put your feet on the table.

PRUDENCE. I didn't put my feet on the table. I put one foot. I was hoping it might get the waiter's attention.

BRUCE. We agree on everything. It's amazing. I'm going to cry again. (*Weeps*)

PRUDENCE. *Please*, you're annoying me.

(HE *continues to cry*)

PRUDENCE. (*Continued*) What is the matter?

BRUCE. I feel you're too dependent. I feel you want me to put up the storm windows. I feel you should do that.

PRUDENCE. I didn't say anything about storm windows.

BRUCE. You're right. I'm wrong. We agree.

PRUDENCE. What kind of childhood did you have?

BRUCE. Nuns. I was taught by nuns. They really ruined me. I don't believe in God anymore. I believe in bran cereal. It helps prevent rectal cancer.

PRUDENCE. Yes, I like bran cereal.

BRUCE. I want to marry you. I feel ready in my life to make a long term commitment. We'll live in Connecticut. We'll have two cars. Bob will live over the garage. Everything will be wonderful.

PRUDENCE. I don't feel ready to make a long term commitment to you. I think you're insane. I'm going to go now. (*Stands*)

BRUCE. Please don't go.

PRUDENCE. I don't think I should stay.

BRUCE. Don't go. They have a salad bar here.

PRUDENCE. Well, maybe for a little longer. (SHE *sits down again*)

BRUCE. You're afraid of life, aren't you?

PRUDENCE. Well...

BRUCE. Your instinct is to run away. You're afraid of feeling of emotion. That's wrong, Prudence, because then you have no passion. Did you see "Equus"? That doctor felt it was better to blind eight horses in a stable with a metal spike than to have no passion. (*Holds his fork*) In my life I'm not going to be afraid to blind the horses, Prudence.

PRUDENCE. You ought to become a veterinarian.

BRUCE. (*Very offended*) You've missed the métaphor.

PRUDENCE. I haven't missed the metaphor. I made a joke.

BRUCE. You just totally missed the metaphor. I could never love someone who missed the metaphor.

PRUDENCE. Someone should have you committed.

BRUCE. I'm not the one afraid of commitment. You are.

PRUDENCE. Oh, dry up.

BRUCE. I was going to give you a fine dinner and then take you to see "The Tree of Wooden Clogs" and then home to my place for sexual intercourse, but now I think you should leave.

PRUDENCE. You're not rejecting me, buddy. I'm rejecting you. You're a real first-class idiot.

BRUCE. And you're a castrating, frigid-bitch!

(SHE *throws a glass of water in his face;* HE *throws water back in her face.* THEY *sit there for a moment, spent of anger, wet*)

PRUDENCE. Absolutely nothing seems to get that waiter's attention, does it?

(BRUCE *shakes his head "no".* THEY *sit there, sadly*)

LIGHTS FADE

ACT I

Scene 2

Psychologist's office. DR. STUART FRAMINGHAM. *Very masculine, a bit of a bully, wears boots, jeans, a tweed sports jacket, open sports shirt. Maybe has a beard.*

STUART. (*Speaking into intercom*) You can send the next patient in now, Betty.

(*Enter* PRUDENCE. SHE *sits*)

STUART. (*Continued. After a moment*) So, what's on your mind this week?

PRUDENCE. Oh I don't know. I had that Catherine the Great dream again.

STUART. Yeah?

PRUDENCE. Oh I don't know. Maybe it isn't Catherine the Great. It's really more like National Velvet.

STUART. What do you associate to National Velvet?

PRUDENCE. Oh I don't know. Childhood.

STUART. Yes?

PRUDENCE. I guess I miss childhood where one could look to a horse for emotional satisfaction rather than a person. I mean, a horse never disappointed me.

STUART. You feel disappointed in people?

PRUDENCE. Well, every man I try to have a relationship with turns out to be crazy. And the ones that aren't crazy are dull. But maybe it's me. Maybe I'm really looking for faults just so I won't ever have a successful relationship. Like Michael last year. Maybe he was just fine, and I made up faults that he didn't have. Maybe I do it to myself. What do you think?

STUART. What I think doesn't matter. What do you think?

PRUDENCE. But what do *you* think?

STUART. It's not my place to say.

PRUDENCE. (*Irritated*) Oh never mind. I don't want to talk about it.

STUART. I see. (*Makes a note*)

PRUDENCE. (*Noticing* HE's *making notes; to make up:*) I did answer one of those ads.

STUART. Oh?

PRUDENCE. Yes.

STUART. How did it work out?

PRUDENCE. Very badly. The guy was a jerk. He talked about my breasts, he has a male lover, and he wept at the table. It was really ridiculous. I should have known better.

STUART. Well, you can always come back to me, babe. I'll light your fire for you anytime.

PRUDENCE. Stuart, I've told you you can't talk to me that way if I'm to stay in therapy with you.

STUART. You're mighty attractive when you're angry.

PRUDENCE. Stuart . . . Dr. Framingham, many women who have been seduced by their psychiatrists take them to court. . .

STUART. Yeah, but you wanted it, baby. . .

PRUDENCE. How could I have "wanted" it? One of our topics has been that I don't know what I want.

STUART. Yeah, but you wanted that, baby.

PRUDENCE. Stop calling me baby. Really, I must be out of my mind to keep seeing you. (*Pause*) Obviously you can't be my therapist after we've had an affair.

STUART. Two lousy nights aren't an affair.

PRUDENCE. You never said they were lousy.

STUART. They were great. You were great. I was great. Wasn't I, baby? It was the fact that it was only two nights that was lousy.

PRUDENCE. Dr. Framingham, it's the common belief that it is wrong for therapists and their patients to have sex together.

STUART. Not in California.

PRUDENCE. We are not in California.

STUART. We could move there. Buy a house, get a jacuzzi.

PRUDENCE. Stuart...Dr. Framingham, we're not right for one another. I feel you have masculinity problems. I hate your belt buckle. I didn't really even like you in bed.

STUART. I'm great in bed.

PRUDENCE. (*With some hesitation*) You have problems with premature ejaculation.

STUART. Listen, honey, there's nothing premature about it. Our society is paced quickly, we all have a lot of things to do. I ejaculate quickly on purpose.

PRUDENCE. I don't believe you.

STUART. Fuck you, cunt.

PRUDENCE. (*Stands*) Obviously I need to find a new therapist.

STUART. Okay, okay. I lost my temper. I'm sorry. But I'm human. Prudence, that's what you have to learn. People *are* human. You keep looking for perfection, you need to learn to accept imperfection. I can help you with that.

PRUDENCE. Maybe I really should sue you. I mean, I don't think you should have a license.

STUART. Prudence, you're avoiding the issue. The issue is you, not me. You're unhappy, you can't find a relationship you like, you don't like your job, you don't like the world. You *need* my help. I mean, don't get hung up on who should have a license. The issue is I can help you fit into the world. (*Very sincerely, sensitively*) Really I can. Don't run away.

PRUDENCE. (*Sits*) I don't think I believe you.

STUART. That's okay. We can work on that.

PRUDENCE. I don't know. I really don't think you're a good therapist. But the others are probably worse, I'm afraid.

STUART. They are. They're much worse. Really I'm very nice. I *like* women. Most men don't.

PRUDENCE. I'm getting one of my headaches again. (*Holds her forehead*)

STUART. Do you want me to massage your neck?

PRUDENCE. Please don't touch me.

STUART. Okay, okay. (*Pause*) Any other dreams?

PRUDENCE. No.

STUART. Perhaps we should analyze why you didn't like the man you met through the personal ad.

PRUDENCE. I...I...don't want to talk anymore today. I want to go home.

STUART. You can never go home again.

PRUDENCE. Perhaps not. But I can return to my apartment. You're making my headache worse.

STUART. I think we should finish the session. I think it's important.

PRUDENCE. I just can't talk anymore.

STUART. We don't have to talk. But we have to stay in the room.

PRUDENCE. How much longer?

STUART. (*Looks at watch*) 30 minutes.

PRUDENCE. Alright. But I'm not going to talk anymore.

STUART. Okay.

(*Pause;* THEY *stare at one another*)

STUART. (*Continued*) You're very beautiful when you're upset.

PRUDENCE. Please don't you talk either.

(THEY *stare at each other; lights dim*)

ACT I

Scene 3

The office of CHARLOTTE WALLACE. *Probably reddish hair, bright clothing; a Snoopy dog on her desk. If there are walls in the set around her, they have drawings done by children.*

CHARLOTTE. (*Into intercom*) You may send the next

patient in, Marcia. (SHE *arranges herself at her desk, smiles in anticipation*)

(*Enter* BRUCE. HE *sits*)

    CHARLOTTE. (*Continued*) Hello.
    BRUCE. Hello. (*Pause*) Should I just begin?
    CHARLOTTE. Would you like to begin?
    BRUCE. I threw a glass of water at someone in a restaurant.
    CHARLOTTE. Did you?
    BRUCE. Yes.
    CHARLOTTE. Did they get all wet?
    BRUCE. Yes.

(*Silence*)

    CHARLOTTE. (*Points to child's drawing*) Did I show you this drawing?
    BRUCE. I don't remember. They all look alike.
    CHARLOTTE. It was drawn by an emotionally disturbed three year old. His parents beat him every morning after breakfast. Orange juice, Toast, Special K.
    BRUCE. Uh huh.
    CHARLOTTE. Do you see the point I'm making?
    BRUCE. Yes, I do, sort of. (*Pause*) What point are you making?
    CHARLOTTE. Well, the point is that when a porpoise first comes to me, it is often immediately clear...Did I say porpoise? What word do I want? Porpoise. Pompous. Pom Pom. Paparazzi. Polyester. Pollywog.

Olley olley oxen free. Patient. I'm sorry, I mean patient. Now what was I saying?

BRUCE. Something about when a patient comes to you.

CHARLOTTE. (*Slightly irritated*) Well, give me more of a clue.

BRUCE. Something about the child's drawing and when a patient comes to you?

CHARLOTTE. Yes. No, I need more. Give me more of a hint.

BRUCE. I don't know.

CHARLOTTE. Oh I hate this, when I forget what I'm saying. Oh, damn. Oh, damn damn damn. Well, we'll just have to forge on. You say something for a while, and I'll keep trying to remember what I was saying. (*She moves her lips*)

BRUCE. (*After a bit*) Do you want me to talk?

CHARLOTTE. Would you like to talk?

BRUCE. I had an answer to the ad I put in.

CHARLOTTE. Ad?

BRUCE. Personal ad.

CHARLOTTE. (*Remembering, happy*) Oh, yes. Personal ad. I told you that was how the first Mr. Wallace and I met. Oh yes. I love personal ads. They're so basic. Did it work out for you?

BRUCE. Well, I liked her, and I tried to be emotionally open with her. I even let myself cry.

CHARLOTTE. Good for you!

BRUCE. But she didn't like me. And then she threw water in my face.

CHARLOTTE. Oh, dear. Oh, I'm sorry. One has to be so brave to be emotionally open and vulnerable. Oh, you poor thing. I'm going to give you a hug. (SHE *hugs him and kisses him with her Snoopy doll*) What did you do when she threw water in your face?

BRUCE. I threw it back in her face.

CHARLOTTE. Oh good for you! Bravo! (SHE *barks for Snoopy and bounces him up and down*) Ruff ruff ruff! Oh, I feel you getting so much more emotionally expressive since you've been in therapy, I'm proud of you.

BRUCE. Maybe it was my fault. I probably came on too strong.

CHARLOTTE. Uh, life is so difficult. I know when I met the second Mr. Wallace...you know, it's so strange, all my husbands have had the same surname of Wallace, this has been a theme in my own analysis...Well, when I met the second Mr. Wallace, I got a filing cabinet caught in my throat...I don't mean a filing cabinet. What do I mean? Filing cabinet, frying pan, frog's eggs, faculty wives, frankincense, fornication, follies bergère, falling falling fork, fish fork, fish bone. I got a fish bone caught in my throat. (*Smiles.*)

BRUCE. And did you get it out?

CHARLOTTE. Oh yes. Then we got married, and we had quite a wonderful relationship for a while, but then he started to see this fish wife and we broke up. I don't mean fish wife, I mean waitress. Is that a word, waitress?

BRUCE. Yes. Woman who works in a restaurant.

CHARLOTTE. No, she didn't work in a restaurant, she worked in a department store. Sales...lady. That's what she was.

BRUCE. That's too bad.

CHARLOTTE. He was buying a gift for me, and then

he ran off with the saleslady. He never even gave me the gift, he just left me a note. And then I was so very alone for a while. (*Cries. After a bit, he gives her a hug and a few kisses from the Snoopy doll. She is suitably grateful*) I'm afraid I'm taking up too much of your session. I'll knock a few dollars off the bill. You talk for a while, I'm getting tired anyway.

BRUCE. Well, so I'm sort of afraid to put another ad in the paper since seeing how this one worked out.

CHARLOTTE. Oh, don't be afraid! Never be afraid to risk, *to risk*! I've told you about "Equus", haven't I? That doctor, Doctor Dysart, with whom I greatly identify, saw that it was better to risk madness and to blind horses with a metal spike, then to be safe and conventional and dull. Ecc, ecc, equus! Naaaaaaaay! (*For Snoopy*) Ruff ruff ruff!

BRUCE. So you think I should put in another ad?

CHARLOTTE. Yes I do. But this time, we need an ad that will get someone more exceptional, someone who can appreciate your uniqueness.

BRUCE. In what ways am I unique? (*Sort of pleased*)

CHALOTTE. Oh I don't know, the usual ways. Now let's see. (*Writing on pad*) White male, 30 to 35, 6'2" no—6'5", green eyes, Pulitzer Prize-winning author, into Kierkegaard, Mahler, Joan Didion and sex, seeks similar-minded attractive female for unique encounters. Sense of humor a must. Write box whatever whatever. There, that should catch you someone excellent. Why don't you take this out to the office, and my dirigible will type it up for you. I don't mean dirigible, I mean Saskatchewan.

BRUCE. Secretary.

CHARLOTTE. Yes, that's what I mean.

BRUCE. You know we haven't mentioned how my putting these ads in the paper for women is making Bob feel. He's real hostile about it.

CHARLOTTE. Who's Bob?

BRUCE. He's the guy I've been living with for a year.

CHARLOTTE. Bob. Oh dear. I'm sorry. I thought you were someone else for this whole session. You're not Thomas Norton?

BRUCE. No, I'm Bruce Lathrop.

CHARLOTTE. Oh yes. Bruce and Bob. It all comes back now. Well I'm very sorry. But this is a good ad anyway, I think, so just bring it out to my dirigible, and then come on back in and we'll talk about something else for a while. I know, I mean secretary. Sometimes I think I should get my blood sugar checked.

BRUCE. Alright, thank you, Mrs. Wallace.

CHARLOTTE. See you next week.

BRUCE. I thought you wanted me to come right back to finish the session.

CHARLOTTE. Oh yes, see you in a few minutes.

(HE *exits*)

CHARLOTTE. (*Continued*) (*Into intercom*) Marcia, dear, send in the next porpoise please. Wait, I don't mean porpoise, I mean . . . pony, pekinese, parka, penis, no not that. I'm sorry, Marcia, I'll buzz back when I think of it. (*She moves her lips, trying to remember. Lights dim*)

ACT I

Scene 4

A restaurant again. BRUCE *waiting, looking at his watch. After a bit enter* PRUDENCE.

PRUDENCE. *(Sees Bruce)* Oh.

BRUCE. Hello again.

PRUDENCE. Hello.

BRUCE. Odd coincidence.

PRUDENCE. Yes.

BRUCE. *(Stands)* Are you answering an ad again?

PRUDENCE. Well, yes, I am.

BRUCE. Me too. I mean I put one in again.

PRUDENCE. Yes, well...I think I'll wait over here. Excuse me. (PRUDENCE *sits at another table; after a bit he comes over.*) Yes?

BRUCE. I'm afraid it's crossed my mind that you answered my ad again.

PRUDENCE. I would not be so stupid as to answer the same ad twice.

BRUCE. I changed my ad.

(SHE *stares at him*)

BRUCE. I was hoping to get a different sort of person.

PRUDENCE. Are you then the Pulitzer Prize winning

author, 6'5", who likes Kierkegaard, Mahler, and Joan Didion?

BRUCE. Yes I am. Sorry.

PRUDENCE. I see. Well that was a ludicrous list of people to like anyway, it serves me right. I feel very embarrassed.

BRUCE. Don't be embarrassed. We're all human.

PRUDENCE. I see no reason not to be embarrassed at being human.

BRUCE. You should be in therapy.

PRUDENCE. I am in therapy.

BRUCE. It hasn't worked.

PRUDENCE. Thank you very much. Do you think we're the only two people who answer these ads?

BRUCE. I doubt it. Maybe we're fated.

PRUDENCE. Jinxed seems more like it.

BRUCE. You think you're unlucky, don't you? In general, I mean. (HE *sits down*)

PRUDENCE. You're going to sit down, are you?

BRUCE. Well, what else should I do? Go home to Bob?

PRUDENCE. Oh yes. How is Bob?

BRUCE. He's kind of grumpy these days.

PRUDENCE. Perhaps he's getting his period.

BRUCE. I don't know much about menstruation. Tell me about it.

PRUDENCE. (*Stares at him*) Yes, I do think I'm unlucky.

BRUCE. What?

PRUDENCE. In answer to your question. I mean, I am attractive, aren't I? I mean, without being conceited, I know I'm *fairly* attractive. I mean, I'm not within the world's 2 per cent mutants...

BRUCE. I don't think you're a mutant at all. I mean, I think you're very attractive.

PRUDENCE. Yes, well, I don't know if I can really credit your opinion. You're sort of a crackpot, aren't you?

BRUCE. You really don't like me, do you?

PRUDENCE. I don't know you really. Well, no, I probably don't like you.

BRUCE. Well I don't like you either.

PRUDENCE. Well, fine. It was delightful to see you again. Goodbye. (*Starts to leave.* HE *starts to cry, but tries to muffle it more than usual.*) I really hate it when you cry. You're much too *large* to cry.

BRUCE. I'm sorry, it's not you. Something was just coming up for me. Some childhood something.

PRUDENCE. Yes, I miss childhood.

BRUCE. I thought you were leaving.

PRUDENCE. (*Sits*) Alright, I want to ask you something. Why did you put that ad in the paper? I mean, if you're living with this person named Bob, why are you trying to meet a woman?

BRUCE. I want to be open to all experiences.

PRUDENCE. Well that sounds all very well, but surely you can't just turn on and off sexual preference.

BRUCE. I don't have to turn it on or off. I prefer both sexes.

PRUDENCE. I don't know, I just find that so difficult to believe.

BRUCE. But why would I be here with you if I weren't interested in you?

PRUDENCE. You might be trying to murder me. Or punish your mother.

BRUCE. Or I might just be trying to reach out and touch someone.

PRUDENCE. That's the slogan of Coke or Dr. Pepper, I think.

BRUCE. The telephone company actually. But it's a good slogan. I mean, isn't that what we're all trying to do, reach out to another person? I mean, I put an ad in a newspaper, after all, and you answered it.

PRUDENCE. I know. It's very hard to meet people. I mean I do meet people at the magazine. I met Shaun Cassidy last week. Of course, he's too young for me.

BRUCE. Bob really likes Shaun Cassidy.

PRUDENCE. Oh, I'll have to try to set them up.

BRUCE. I don't think your therapist is helping you at all.

PRUDENCE. Well I think yours must be a maniac.

BRUCE. My therapist says you have to be willing to go out on a limb, to risk, to risk!

PRUDENCE. My therapist says... (*at a loss*) I have to settle for imperfection.

BRUCE. I know it's unconventional to be bisexual. My wife Sally didn't deal with it at all well.

PRUDENCE. You were married?

BRUCE. For six years. I married this girl Sally I knew all through grammar school and everything. She was runner-up for the homecoming queen.

PRUDENCE. I didn't go to the prom. I read "Notes From The Underground" instead.

BRUCE. You should have gone to the prom.

PRUDENCE. I don't like proms. Why did you and Sally break up?

BRUCE. Well, I didn't understand about bisexuality

then. I thought the fact that I wanted to sleep with the man who came to read the gas meter meant I was queer.

PRUDENCE. I'm never home when they come to read the gas meter.

BRUCE. And so then Sally found out I was sleeping with the gas man, and she got real angry and we got a divorce.

PRUDENCE. Well I guess if you're homecoming queen runner-up you don't expect those sorts of problems.

BRUCE. You haven't been married, have you?

PRUDENCE. (*Uncomfortable*) No.

BRUCE. Has there been anyone serious?

PRUDENCE. I have two cats. Serious, let's see. Well, about a year and a half ago I lived for six months with this aging preppie named Michael.

BRUCE. (*Pleased—a connection*) I'm an aging preppie.

PRUDENCE. Yes I know. Michael was a lawyer, and...

BRUCE. I'm a lawyer.

PRUDENCE. (*Registers this fact, then goes on*) And he was very smart, and very nice; and I should've been happy with him, and I don't know why I wasn't. And he was slightly allergic to my cats, so I broke it off.

BRUCE. And you haven't gone out with anyone since?

PRUDENCE. Well I do go out with people, but it never seems to work out.

BRUCE. Maybe you're too hard on them.

PRUDENCE. Well should I pretend someone is wonderful if I think they're stupid or crazy?

BRUCE. Well no, but maybe you judge everybody too quickly.

PRUDENCE. Well perhaps. But how many nights would you give David Berkowitz?

BRUCE. You went out with David Berkowitz?

PRUDENCE. No. It was a rhetorical question.

BRUCE. You must ask yourself what you want. Do you want to be married?

PRUDENCE. I have no idea. It's so confusing. I know when I was a little girl, Million Dollar Movie showed this film called "Every Girl Should Be Married" every night for seven days. It was this dumb comedy about this infantile girl played by Betsy Drake who wants to be married to this pediatrician played by Cary Grant who she sees in a drug store. She sees him for two minutes, and she wants to move in and have babies with him. And he finds her totally obnoxious, but then at the end of the movie suddenly says, "You're right, you're adorable," and then they get married. (*Looks baffled by the stupidity of it all*)

BRUCE. Well it was a comedy.

PRUDENCE. And what confused me further was that the actress Betsy Drake did in fact marry Cary Grant in real life. Of course, it didn't last, and he married several other people, and then later Dyan Cannon said he was insane and took LSD and so maybe one wouldn't want to be married to him at all. But if it's no good being married to Cary Grant, who is it good being married to?

BRUCE. I don't know.

PRUDENCE. Neither do I.

BRUCE. Well you should give things time. First impressions can be wrong. And maybe Dyan Cannon was the problem. Maybe anyone married to her would take LSD. Maybe Cary Grant is still terrific.

PRUDENCE. Well he's too old for me anyway. Shaun Cassidy's too young, and Cary Grant's too old.

BRUCE. I'm the right age.

PRUDENCE. Yes I guess you are.

BRUCE. And you haven't left. You said you were leaving but then you stayed.

PRUDENCE. Well it's not particularly meaningful. I was just curious why you put the ad in the paper.

BRUCE. Why did you answer it?

PRUDENCE. I don't wish to analyze my behavior on the issue.

BRUCE. You're so afraid of things. I feel this overwhelming urge to help you. We can look into the abyss together.

PRUDENCE. Please don't say pretentious things. I get a rash.

BRUCE. (*Depressed*) You're right. I guess I am pretentious.

PRUDENCE. Well I really am too hard on people.

BRUCE. No you're probably right to dislike me. Sally hates me. I mean, sometimes I hear myself and I understand why no one likes me.

PRUDENCE. Please don't be so hard on yourself on my account. Everyone's stupid, so you're just like everyone else.

(HE *stares at her*)

PRUDENCE. (*Continued*) I'm sorry, that sounded terrible. I'm stupid too. We're all stupid.

BRUCE. It's human to be stupid. (*Sings romantically*) There's a somebody I'm longing duh duh, Duh duh duh duh, duh duh duh duh... (*Stops singing*)

PRUDENCE. (*Sings*) Someone to watch... (*Realizes SHE's singing alone*) Oh I didn't realize you were stopping.

BRUCE. Sorry. I didn't realize you were...starting.

PRUDENCE. Yes. Stupid of me to like that song.

BRUCE. It's a pretty song.

PRUDENCE. Well I guess it is.

BRUCE. I want to say something. I like you.

PRUDENCE. (*Surprised anyone could like her*) You do?

BRUCE. I like women who are independent-minded, who don't look to a man to do all their thinking for them. I like women who are persons.

PRUDENCE. Well you sound like you were coached by Betty Friedan, but otherwise that's a nice sentiment. Of course, a woman who was independent-minded wouldn't like the song "Someone To Watch Over Me."

BRUCE. We have to allow for contradictions in ourselves. Nobody is just one thing.

PRUDENCE. (*Serious*) That's very true. That wasn't a crackpot comment at all.

BRUCE. I know it wasn't. And just because I'm a crackpot on some things doesn't mean I'm a total crackpot.

PRUDENCE. Right. You're a partial crackpot.

BRUCE. You could be a crackpot too if you let yourself go.

PRUDENCE. That wasn't what I was attempting to do when I got up this morning.

BRUCE. To risk, to risk! Do you like me?

PRUDENCE. Well, I don't know. I don't really know you yet.

BRUCE. Do you want to get to know me?

PRUDENCE. Well I don't know. Maybe I shouldn't. I mean, we did meet through a personal ad, you don't have a Pulitzer Prize...

BRUCE. I have a membership in the New York Health and Racquet Club.

PRUDENCE. Well similiar, but not the same thing.

BRUCE. As a member I can get you a discount.

PRUDENCE. I don't know if I'm ready to exercise yet. I'm thinking about it, but I'm cautious still.

BRUCE. We're getting on, aren't we?

PRUDENCE. Well yes, in a way. (*Smiles warmly; he smiles back; she then looks around*) Do you think maybe they don't have waiters in this restaurant?

BRUCE. Maybe they're on strike. Why don't we go to another restaurant? I know a good Mexican one.

PRUDENCE. I don't like Mexican food, I'm afraid.

BRUCE. Japanese?

PRUDENCE. Well no.

BRUCE. Chinese?

PRUDENCE. Well more than Japanese, but not really.

BRUCE. Where do you want to go?

PRUDENCE. Well could we go to an American Restaurant? I know I'm very dull, but I didn't even like vanilla ice cream when I was a child. I was afraid of it.

BRUCE. That's a significant statement you've just made.

PRUDENCE. It does sound pathological, doesn't it?

BRUCE. Don't be afraid to sound pathological. That's what I've learned from my therapy so far.

PRUDENCE. I don't think I've learned much from mine yet.

BRUCE. Maybe I can help you. We can look into the abyss together. Oh that's right, you didn't like it when I said that before.

PRUDENCE. That's alright. I'll look into the abyss for one evening.

BRUCE. Oh you're becoming more open. Good for you. Ruff, ruff, ruff!

PRUDENCE. (*Very taken aback*) I'm sorry?

BRUCE. (*Very embarrassed*) Oh, my therapist barks. For encouragement.

PRUDENCE. Ah, of course.

BRUCE. (*Back to getting to know her*) Now tell me about your fear of vanilla ice cream.

PRUDENCE. (*As they walk out*) Well, I had gotten very used to baby food, and I also liked junket, but there was something about the *texture* of vanilla ice cream . . .

(THEY *exit*)

ACT I

Scene 5

DR. STUART FRAMINGHAM's *office again.*

STUART. (*On phone*) Hiya, babe, it's me. Whatcha doin'? Oh, I'm just waiting for my next patient. Last night was great, wasn't it? It was great. What? So quickly. What is it with you women? You read some

goddamned sex manual and then you think sex is
supposed to go on for hours or something. I mean, if
you're so frigid you can't get excited in a couple of
minutes, that's not my problem. No it isn't. Well,
fuck you too. (*Hangs up*) Jesus God. (*Into intercom*)
Betty, you can send in the next patient.

(*Enter* PRUDENCE)

STUART. (*Continued*) Hello.
PRUDENCE. Hello.
STUART. What's on your mind this week?
PRUDENCE. Nothing.
STUART. (*Furious*) Goddam it. I don't feel like drag-
ging the words out of you this week. Talk, damn it.
PRUDENCE. What?
STUART. You pay me to listen, so TALK! (*Pause*)
I'm sorry, I'm on edge today. And all my patients
are this way. None of them talk. Well this one guy
talks, but he talks in Yiddish a lot, and I don't know
what the fuck he's saying.
PRUDENCE. Well you should tell him that you don't
understand.
STUART. Don't tell me how to run my business! Be-
sides, we're here to talk about you. How was your
week? Another series of lonely, loveless evenings?
I'm still here, babe.
PRUDENCE. Don't call me babe. No, I've had some
pleasant evenings actually.
STUART. You have?
PRUDENCE. Yes I have.
STUART. You been answering ads in the paper again?

PRUDENCE. Well, yes actually.

STUART. That's a slutty thing to do.

PRUDENCE. As a therapist you are utterly ridiculous.

STUART. I'm just kidding you. You shouldn't lose your sense of humor, babe, especially when you're in a promiscuous stage.

PRUDENCE. I am not promiscuous.

STUART. There's nothing wrong with being promiscuous. We're all human.

PRUDENCE. Yes, we are all human.

STUART. So who is this guy? Have you slept with him?

PRUDENCE. Dr. Framingham....

STUART. Really, I gotta know for therapy.

PRUDENCE. Yes, we have slept together. Once. I wasn't really planning to, but...

STUART. Is he better than me?

PRUDENCE. Stuart...

STUART. No really. You liked him better? Tell me.

PRUDENCE. Yes I did. Much better.

STUART. I suppose he took his time. I suppose it lasted just hours. That's sick! Wanting sex to take a long time is sick!

PRUDENCE. Well he was attentive to how I felt, if that's what you mean.

STUART. So this fellow was a real success, huh?

PRUDENCE. Success and failure are not particularly likeable terms to describe sexual outings, but if you must, yes, it was successful. Probably his experiences with men have made him all that better as a lover.

STUART. What?

PRUDENCE. He's bisexual.

STUART. (*Starting to feel on the winning team again*) Oh yeah?

PRUDENCE. So he tells me. Masters and Johnson say that homosexuals make much more responsive sex partners anyway.

STUART. BULLSHIT! You are talking such bullshit! I understand you now. You're obviously afraid of a real man, and so you want to cuddle with some eunuch who isn't a threat to you. I understand all this now!

PRUDENCE. There's no need to call him a eunuch. A eunuch has no testicles.

STUART. I GOT BALLS, BABY!

PRUDENCE. I am so pleased for you.

STUART. You're afraid of men!

PRUDENCE. I am not afraid of men.

STUART. You're a fag hag. (*To himself*) I gotta write that down. (*Writes that down, makes further notes*)

PRUDENCE. Look, I admit I find this man's supposed bisexuality confusing and I don't quite believe it. But what are my options? A two minute roll in the hay with you, where you make no distinction between sexual intercourse and push-ups; and then a happy evening of admiring your underarm hair and your belt buckles? (*Irritated*) What are you writing?

STUART. (*Reading from his pad*) I'd like to give this patient electro-shock therapy. I'd like to put this patient in a clothes dryer until her hair falls out. I'd like to tie her to the radiator and... (*Stops, hears himself, looks stricken*)

PRUDENCE. I think this is obviously my last session.

STUART. No, no, no. You're taking me seriously. I'm

testing you. It was a test. I was just putting you on.

PRUDENCE. For what purpose?

STUART. I can't tell you. It would interfere with your therapy.

PRUDENCE. You call this therapy?

STUART. We're reaching the richest part of our therapy and already I see results. But I think you're entering a very uncharted part of your life just now, and so you must stay with your therapy. You're going out with homosexuals, God knows what you're going to do next. Now I'm very serious. I'm holding out the lifeline. Don't turn away.

PRUDENCE. Well I'll think about it, but I don't know.

STUART. You're a very sick woman, and you mustn't be without a therapist even for a day.

PRUDENCE. (*Not taken in by this; wanting to leave without a scene*) Is the session over yet?

STUART. We have 30 more minutes.

PRUDENCE. Could I go early?

STUART. I think it's important that we finish out the session.

PRUDENCE. I'd like to go.

STUART. Please, please, please, please...

PRUDENCE. Alright, alright. For God's sake.

(THEY *settle down, back in their chairs*)

STUART. When are you seeing this person again? I'm asking as your therapist.

PRUDENCE. Tonight. He's making dinner for us.

STUART. *He's* making dinner?

PRUDENCE. He says he likes to cook.

STUART. I don't think I need say anything more.
PRUDENCE. I don't think you do either.

(THEY *stare at one another; lights dim*)

ACT I

Scene 6

BRUCE's *apartment.* BRUCE *fiddling with pillows, on couch, looking at watch, etc. Doorbell.* BRUCE *lets in* PRUDENCE.

BRUCE. Hi. Come on in.
PRUDENCE. Hello. (THEY *kiss*) I brought some wine.
BRUCE. Oh thanks.
PRUDENCE. You have a nice apartment.
BRUCE. Thanks.
PRUDENCE. It looks just like my apartment.
BRUCE. Yeah I guess it does.
PRUDENCE. And like my office at the magazine. And like the lobby at the bank. Everything looks alike.
BRUCE. Yes, I guess it does.
PRUDENCE. I'm sorry, I'm just rattling on.
BRUCE. That's alright. Sit down.

(THEY *sit*)

BRUCE. Can I get you a drink?

PRUDENCE. Ummm, I don't know.

BRUCE. Do you want one?

PRUDENCE. I don't know. Do you want one?

BRUCE. Well I thought I might have some Perrier.

PRUDENCE. Oh that sounds good.

BRUCE. Two Perriers?

PRUDENCE. Well, do you have Poland water?

BRUCE. I think I do. Wait here. I'll be right back. (BRUCE *exits. After a moment* BOB *enters.* BOB *sees* PRUDENCE, *is rattled, ill at ease*)

BOB. Oh. You're here already. I...didn't hear the bell ring.

PRUDENCE. Oh. Hello. Are you Bob?

BOB. Yes. (*At a loss, making an odd joke*) And you must be Marie of Roumania.

PRUDENCE. I'm Prudence.

BOB. Yes, I know. (*At a loss how to get out of room*) Is Bruce in the kitchen?

PRUDENCE. Yes.

BOB. Oh. (*Starts to go there; stops*) Oh, well, never mind. When he comes out would you tell him I want to see him in the other room?

PRUDENCE. Alright.

BOB. Excuse me. (*Exits back to bedroom presumably. Enter* BRUCE *with two glasses of sparkling water*)

BRUCE. Well here we are. One Perrier, and one Poland water.

PRUDENCE. I thought you said Bob was away.

BRUCE. Oh, you met Bob already? Yes, he *was* going away, but then he changed his mind and I'd already bought the lamb chops.

PRUDENCE. You mean he's going to be here all through dinner?

BRUCE. Oh I don't think so. He said he was going to his mother's for dinner. He has a very funny mother. She's sort of like Auntie Mame.

PRUDENCE. Oh yes?

BRUCE. Now don't let Bob upset you.

PRUDENCE. Well he seemed very uncomfortable. He asked me if I was Marie of Roumania.

BRUCE. Oh, he says that to everyone. Don't take it personally. (*Raising drink*) Well, cheers.

PRUDENCE. (*Remembering*) Oh. He said he wanted to see you in the other room.

BRUCE. Oh. Well, alright. I'll just be a minute. Here, why don't you read a magazine?

PRUDENCE. "People," how nice.

BRUCE. Be right back.

(*Exits.* PRUDENCE *reads magazine uncomfortably, and tastes his Perrier water to compare it with her Poland water. We and she start to hear the following offstage argument; initially it's just a buzz of voices but it grows into anger and shouting.* PRUDENCE *looks very uncomfortable*)

BRUCE. (*Offstage*) This isn't the time to talk about this, Bob.

BOB. (*Offstage*) Well, when is the time?

BRUCE. (*Offstage*) We can talk about this later.

BOB. (*Offstage*) That's obviously very convenient for you.

BRUCE. (*Offstage*) Bob, this isn't the time to talk about this.

BOB. (*Offstage*) Well when *is* the time?

BRUCE. (*Offstage*) Come on, Bob, calm down. (*Softer*) Now I told you this doesn't have anything to do with us.

BOB. (*Offstage. Very angry*) Oh God!

BRUCE. (*Offstage*) I'm sick of this behavior, Bob!

BOB. (*Offstage*) Well I'm sick of it too!

(*There is a crash of something breaking. Pause. Then re-enter* BRUCE)

BRUCE. Everything's fine now. (*Pause*) We broke a vase. Well, Bob broke it.

PRUDENCE. Maybe I should go.

BRUCE. No, everything's fine now. Once Bob vents his anger then everything's fine again.

PRUDENCE. I thought you told me that Bob didn't mind your seeing me, and that the two of you had broken up anyway.

BRUCE. Well, I lied. Sorry. Some members of Bob's group therapy wrote me a note saying they thought if I wanted to see women, I should just go on and see women, and so I just sort of presumed they'd convince Bob eventually, but I guess they haven't yet.

PRUDENCE. They wrote you a letter?

BRUCE. It's a very intense group Bob is in. They're always visiting each other in the hospital and things.

PRUDENCE. But what shall we do about this evening?

BRUCE. I think you and Bob will really like one another once you get past this initial discomfort. And besides, I'm sure he'll be going to his mother's in a little while.

PRUDENCE. Maybe we should go to a restaurant.

BRUCE. No really I bought the lamb chops. It'll be fine. Oh my God, the rice. I have to go see about the rice. It's wild rice; well, rice-a-roni. I have to go see about browning it. I won't be a minute.

PRUDENCE. No, no, don't leave...

BRUCE. It's alright. (*As* HE *leaves*) Bob will come talk to you... (*Exits*)

PRUDENCE. (*As* SHE *sees* HE's *gone*) I know...Oh dear.

(*Enter* BOB)

BOB. Hello again.

PRUDENCE. Oh hi.

BOB. I didn't mean to make you uncomfortable about Marie of Roumania. It's just something I say.

PRUDENCE. Oh that's alright.

BOB. (*Offering it as information*) I just broke a vase.

PRUDENCE. (*Being pleasant*) Oh yes, I thought I heard something.

BOB. Bruce says that I will like you if I can just get past my initial hostility.

PRUDENCE. Oh. Well I hope so.

BOB. Bruce is really a very conflicted person. I really suffer a lot dealing with him.

PRUDENCE. Oh I'm sorry.

BOB. And now this latest thing of having women traipse through here at all hours.

PRUDENCE. Ah.

BOB. Did you ever see the movie "Sunday Bloody Sunday"?

PRUDENCE. No I didn't. I meant to.

BOB. Well I sure wish Bruce had never seen it. It had a big effect on him. It's all about this guy played by Murray Head who's having an affair with Peter Finch *and* with Glenda Jackson.

PRUDENCE. Oh. Good actors.

BOB. Yes, well the point is it's a very silly movie because I don't think bisexuality exists, do you?

PRUDENCE. Well it's hard to know really.

BOB. I mean, I think that Bruce is just trying to prove something with all these ads in the paper for women. That's what my mother says about Bruce. She tells me I should just be patient and understanding and that it's just a phase Bruce is going through. I've put a lot of work into this relationship. And it's so difficult meeting new people, it's just thoroughly intimidating.

PRUDENCE. It is hard to meet people.

BOB. I think everyone is basically gay, don't you?

PRUDENCE. Well, no, not really.

BOB. You just say that because you haven't come out yet. I know lots of lesbians who'd like you a lot. I'd be happy to give them your number.

PRUDENCE. Thank you, but no.

(*Enter* BRUCE)

BRUCE. Well I burned the rice. Sorry. We'll just have more salad.

PRUDENCE. Oh that's alright.

BRUCE. So have you two been getting to know one another?

PRUDENCE. Yes.

BOB. (*Truly being conversational, not trying to be*

rude. To BRUCE) Don't you think Prudence would be a big hit in a lesbian bar?

BRUCE. Yes, I guess she would.

BOB. I know Liz Skinner would certainly like her.

BRUCE. Yes, she is Liz's type.

PRUDENCE. Bruce, could I speak to you for a moment please? (*To* BOB) I'm sorry, excuse me.

(BRUCE *and* PRUDENCE *cross to side of room*)

PRUDENCE. Bruce, I'm getting very uncomfortable. Now you told me that Bob wasn't going to be here and that he wasn't jealous about your seeing women, and I don't want to be told which lesbians would like me, so I think maybe I should forget the whole thing and go home.

BRUCE. No please, don't go. Bob needs help to get over his feelings about this, and I'm sure he'll go to his mother's in a little while. So please just be nice to him for a little longer. For our sake.

PRUDENCE. I don't know.

BRUCE. Really, it'll be fine.

PRUDENCE. (*Deciding to try*) All right. All right.

(THEY *return to* BOB)

PRUDENCE. (*On returning, to* BOB) Sorry.

BOB. Don't be sorry. I realize I make you uncomfortable.

PRUDENCE. No, no, really it's not that.

BRUCE. Prudence likes you, Bob. She isn't like the other women you know.

PRUDENCE. Yes, I do...I like lots of men. (*Laughs nervously*)

BOB. We have that in common.

PRUDENCE. Yes... (*Laughs, very uncomfortable*)

BRUCE. (*Making big transition into "conversation"*) So, Prudence, did you finish writing your interview with Joyce De Witt?

BOB. Who's Joyce De Witt?

PRUDENCE. (*Trying to be very friendly*) Oh, she's the brunette actress on the tv show "Three's a Crowd." (*Pause; looks mortified*) I mean, "Three's Company."

(*Long pause.* THEY *all feel awful*)

BRUCE. So, did you finish the article?

PRUDENCE. Yes, I did. Right on time. (*Pause; to* BOB) Bruce tells me your mother is like Auntie Mame.

(BOB *glares at* BRUCE)

PRUDENCE. (*Continued*) Oh, I'm sorry. Was that a bad thing to say?

BOB. It depends on what you mean by Auntie Mame.

PRUDENCE. I don't know. Bruce said it.

BOB. My mother has a certain flair, if that's what he means.

BRUCE. Your mother acts like a transvestite. I'm sorry, she does.

BOB. Just because my mother has a sense of

humor is no reason to accuse her of not being fem-
inine. (*To* PRUDENCE) Don't you agree that women
theoretically can have senses of humor?

PRUDENCE. Yes indeed.

BRUCE. Sense of humor isn't the issue.

PRUDENCE. (*Trying to help conversation*) I've always hated transvestites. It's such a repugnant image
of women.

(BOB *looks disapproving*)

PRUDENCE. (*Continued*) I'm sorry, I don't mean to
imply anything about your mother. I...I liked Jack
Lemmon as a woman in "Some Like It Hot."

BOB. My mother does not resemble Jack Lemmon
in "Some Like It Hot."

PRUDENCE. I'm sure she doesn't. I didn't mean to
imply...

BRUCE. Change the subject, Prudence. This is getting us nowhere.

PRUDENCE. Oh, alright. (*Thinks*) What does Bob do
for a living?

BOB. I'm still in the room.

PRUDENCE. Oh I'm sorry, I know you are. (*Pause*)
What do you do for a living, Bob?

BOB. I'm a pharmacist.

PRUDENCE. Oh really?

BOB. Do you need any pills?

PRUDENCE. No thank you. (*Pause*) Maybe later.

BRUCE. (*To* PRUDENCE) Can I freshen your Poland
water?

PRUDENCE. No thank you. I'm fine. (*Pause*) So

you're a pharmacist.

BOB. Yes.

BRUCE. I wish I hadn't burned the rice. (*Whispers to* PRUDENCE) Say something to him, he's starting to sulk.

PRUDENCE. Ummmm... What exactly is in Tylenol, I wonder.

BOB. That's alright. I realize I'm making everyone uncomfortable. Excuse me. (*Exits*)

PRUDENCE. Really, Bruce, this isn't very fair to me. This is a problem the two of you should work out together.

BRUCE. Well you're right actually. You're always right. That's why I like you so much. (*Moves closer, puts arm around her*)

PRUDENCE. Maybe I should go.

BRUCE. Oh you're too sensitive. Besides, he'll be leaving soon.

(BOB *re-enters*)

BOB. My mother's on the phone.

BRUCE. I didn't hear it ring.

BOB. I called her. (*To* PRUDENCE) She wants to speak to you.

PRUDENCE. I don't understand. I...

BOB. (*Hands her the phone*) Here.

PRUDENCE. (*It's happening too fast to stop*) Hello. Who is this? Oh, hello. Yes. (*Laughs uncomfortably*) Yes, thank you. What? No, I don't want to ruin your son's life. What? No, really, I'm not trying to...

BRUCE. (*Takes phone away from* PRUDENCE; *talks into it*) Now, look, Sadie, I've told you not to meddle in my life. It doesn't do anybody any good when you do, including Bob. Don't sing when I'm talking to you, that's not communication to sing when someone is talking to you. Sadie...Sadie! (*Hands phone to* BOB) She's singing "Rose's Turn" from "Gypsy," it's utterly terrifying.

BOB. Hello, mother.

BRUCE. (*To* PRUDENCE) She's an insane woman.

BOB. Mother, it's me, you can stop singing now. Okay, well, just finish the phrase. (*Listens*)

PRUDENCE. Where's Bob's father?

BRUCE. She killed him.

BOB. That's not funny, Bruce. Okay, mother, wrap the song up now. Yes, I'm alright. Yes, I'll tell them. (*To the* TWO *of them*) My mother thinks you're both very immature. (*Back to phone*) Yes, I think she's a lesbian too.

PRUDENCE. I'm going to go home now.

BRUCE. No, no, I'll fix this. (*Takes phone away from* BOB) Finish this conversation in the other room, Bob. Then please get out of here, as we agreed you would do earlier, so Prudence and I can have our dinner. I mean, we agreed upon this, Bob.

BOB. You mean you agreed upon it.

BRUCE. I've finished with this conversation, Bob. Go in the other room and talk to your mother. (*Listens to phone*) What's she singing now, I don't recognize it?

(BOB *and* BRUCE *both listen to phone*)

BOB. That's "Welcome to Kanagawa" from "Pacific Overtures."

BRUCE. Keep singing, Sadie. Bob is changing phones. It was good hearing from you.

BRUCE. I just don't understand your behavior. I just don't. (*Exits*)

PRUDENCE. Bruce, I can't tell you how uncomfortable I am. Really I must go home, and then the two of you should go to a marriage counselor or something.

BRUCE. I am sorry. I should have protected you from this. (*Listens to phone, hangs it up*)

PRUDENCE. I mean we're only seeing one another casually, and you and Bob have been living together and his mother calls up and she sings...

BRUCE. Prudence, I'm not feeling all that casual anymore. Are you?

PRUDENCE. Well I don't know. I mean, probably yes, it's still casual.

BRUCE. It needn't be.

PRUDENCE. Bruce, I just don't think your life is in order.

BRUCE. Of course it's not. How can life be in order? Life by its very nature is disordered, terrifying. That's why people come together, to face the terrors hand in hand.

PRUDENCE. You're giving me my rash again.

BRUCE. You're so afraid of feeling.

PRUDENCE. Oh, just put the lamb chops on.

BRUCE. I feel very close to you.

(*Enter* BOB *with suitcase. Phone rings*)

BOB. Don't answer it. It's just my mother again. I told her I was checking into a hotel and then jumping out the window. There's just no point in continuing. (*To* PRUDENCE, *sincerely*) I hope you're both very happy...Really.

PRUDENCE. (*Startled, confused*) Thank you.

BRUCE. Bob, come back here. (*Answers phone*) Sadie, we'll call you back. (*Hangs up*) Bob.

BOB. No, go back to your evening. I don't want to stand in your way.

BRUCE. You're just trying to get attention.

BOB. There's just no point in continuing.

(*Phone rings;* BRUCE *answers it*)

BRUCE. It's all right, Sadie, I'll handle this. (*Hangs up*) Bob, people who announce their suicide are just asking for help, isn't that so, Prudence?

PRUDENCE. I really don't know. I think I should leave.

BOB. No, please, I don't want to spoil your dinner.

BRUCE. You're just asking for help. (*Phone rings*) Let's let it ring. Bob, look at me. I want you to get help. Can you hear me? I want you to see my therapist.

BOB. I have my own group therapy.

BRUCE. You need better help than that. Doesn't he, Prudence? (*Answers* p*hone*) It's all right, Sadie, I'm going to call up my therapist right away. (*Hangs up*) Now you just sit down here, Bob, and we're going to call Mrs. Wallace right up. (*To* PRUDENCE) Unless you think your therapist is better.

PRUDENCE. No! Yours would have to be better.

BOB. I don't know what you have against my group therapy. It's been very helpful to me.

BRUCE. Bob, you're trying to kill yourself. That proves to me that group therapy is a failure.

BOB. Suicide is an innate human right.

(*Phone rings*)

BRUCE. (*To* PRUDENCE; *hands her phone*) Will you tell her to stop calling?

PRUDENCE. Hello?

BRUCE. You're not acting logically.

PRUDENCE. No, I don't want to see him dead.

BOB. I simply think I should end my life now. That's logical.

PRUDENCE. Please don't shout at me, Mrs. Lansky.

BRUCE. We have to talk this through.

PRUDENCE. Bruce.

BOB. I don't want to talk it through. (*Sings*) Frere Jacques, Frere Jacques, dormez-vous? dormez-vous? (*Etc., continues on*)

PRUDENCE. Bruce.

BRUCE. Don't sing when I'm talking to you.

PRUDENCE. Bruce.

BRUCE. What is it, Prudence?

PRUDENCE. Please, Mrs. Lansky is yelling at me.

BRUCE. Well she can't hurt you. Yell back.

BOB. (*Takes phone*) Mother, it's alright, I want to die. (*Hands phone back to* PRUDENCE, *goes back to song*) Ding dong ding ding dong ding. Frere Jacques ... (*Continues*)

BRUCE. Bob, you're acting like a baby.

PRUDENCE. No, he's still alive, Mrs. Lansky.

BRUCE. (*Irritated, starts to sing at* BOB) 76 trombones led the big parade, with 110 cornets close behind... (*Continues*)

PRUDENCE. Mrs. Lansky, I'm going to hang up now. Goodbye. Stop yelling. (*Hangs up*)

BOB. (*Stops singing*) Did you hang up on my mother?

(BRUCE *stops too*)

PRUDENCE. (*Really letting him have it*) Oh why don't you just go kill yourself?

(BOB *sits down, stunned. Phone rings*)

PRUDENCE. (*Continued*) (*Answers it*) Oh shut up! (*Hangs up*) I am very uninterested in being involved in this nonsense. You're both just making a big overdramatic mess out of everything, and I don't want to watch it anymore.

BRUCE. You're right. Bob, she's right.

BOB. (*Looks up*) She is?

BRUCE. Yes, she is. We're really acting stupid. (*Phone rings.* BRUCE *picks it up, and hangs up immediately. Then he dials*) I'm calling Mrs. Wallace now. I think we really need help.

PRUDENCE. You have her home number?

BRUCE. Yes. She's a really wonderful woman. She gave me her home number after our second session.

PRUDENCE. I slept with my therapist after our second session.

BRUCE. Hello? Uh, is Mrs. Wallace there? Thank you. (*To* THEM) I think that was her husband.

BOB. (*Not defiantly; just for something to do, sings softly*) Frere Jacques, frere Jacques, dormez-vous ... (*Etc.*)

BRUCE. (*Suddenly hearing it*) What do you mean you slept with your therapist?

PRUDENCE. I don't know, I...

BRUCE. (*To* BOB *suddenly, as* MRS. WALLACE *is now on the phone*) Sssssh. (*Into phone*) Hello. Mrs. Wallace? Mrs. Wallace, this is Bruce, we have a bit of an emergency, I wonder if you can help...we're in desperate need of some therapy here...

END ACT I

ACT II

Scene 1

Act I. MRS. WALLACE'S *office, twenty minutes after the end of Act I.* MRS. WALLACE *present, enter* BRUCE *and* BOB.

BRUCE. Hi, it's us.

CHARLOTTE. Hello.

BRUCE. Really, it's so nice of you to see us right away.

CHARLOTTE. That's alright.

BRUCE. Mrs. Wallace, this is Bob Lansky.

CHARLOTTE. Hello.

BOB. Hello.

BRUCE. Well I'm going to leave you two and go have dinner with Prudence.

BOB. You're not going to stay?

BRUCE. Bob, you're the one who's not handling this situation well. Now I haven't eaten all day, and this hasn't been fair to Prudence. (*To* MRS. WALLACE) Now if he gets totally out of control, we're going to be at the Restaurant. I mean that's the name of the restaurant. I mean I could be paged. Otherwise, I'll just see you back at the apartment.

BOB. I thought you wanted her to talk to us together.

BRUCE. Not for the first session. Now you listen to what Mrs. Wallace has to say, and I'll see you later

tonight. (*Gives* BOB *an affectionate hug, then exits.*
BOB *and* MRS. WALLACE *stare at one another for a
while*)

BOB. Should I sit down?

CHARLOTTE. Would you like to sit down?

(HE *sits.* SHE *sits, holds her Snoopy doll*)

BOB. Why are you holding that doll?

CHARLOTTE. Does it bother you that I hold the doll?

BOB. I don't know.

CHARLOTTE. Were you allowed to have dolls as a
child?

BOB. Yes I was. It was trucks I wasn't allowed to
have.

CHARLOTTE. (*Confused*) Great big trucks?

BOB. Toy trucks.

(*Silence*)

CHARLOTTE. Now, what seems to be the matter?

BOB. Bruce seems to be trying to end our relationship.

CHARLOTTE. What do you mean?

BOB. He's been putting these ads in the paper for
women. And now he seems a little serious about this
new one.

CHARLOTTE. Women?

BOB. Women.

CHARLOTTE. And why does this bother you?

BOB. Well, Bruce and I have been living together
for a year. A little more.

CHARLOTTE. Living together?

BOB. Yes.

CHARLOTTE. As roommates?

BOB. Well, if that's the euphemism you prefer.

CHARLOTTE. I prefer nothing. I'm here to help you.

BOB. But you can see the problem.

CHARLOTTE. Well if Bruce should move out, surely you can find another roommate. They advertise in the paper. As a matter of fact, my son is looking for a roommate, he doesn't get on with the present Mr. Wallace. Maybe you could room with him.

BOB. I don't think you've understood. Bruce and I aren't just roommates, you know. I mean, doesn't he talk to you about me in his own therapy?

CHARLOTTE. Let me get his file. (*Looks through her drawers, takes out rope, binoculars, orange juice carton, folders, messy cup board. Laughs*) No, it's not here. Maybe my dirigible knows where it is. (*Pushes button*) Marcia. Oh that's right, she's not in the office now. (*To intercom*) Never mind. Well, I'll have to rely on memory.

BOB. Dirigible?

CHARLOTTE. I'm sorry, did I say dirigible? Now what word did I want?

BOB. Blimp?

CHARLOTTE. (*Not understanding*) Blimp?

BOB. Is the word blimp?

CHARLOTTE. (*Irritated*) No it's nothing like blimp. Now you've made me forget what I was saying. (*Holds her head*) Something about apartments. Oh yes. Did you want to meet my son as a possible roommate?

BOB. I don't understand what you're talking about. Why do you want me to meet your son? Is he gay?

CHARLOTTE. (*Offended*) No he's not gay. What an awful thing to suggest. He just wants to share an apartment with someone. Isn't that what you want?

BOB. No it isn't. I have not come to you for real estate advice. I've come to you because my lover and I are in danger of breaking up.

CHARLOTTE. Lover?

BOB. Your patient, Bruce! The person who was just here. He and I are lovers, don't you know that?

CHARLOTTE. Good God, no!

BOB. What do you mean, Good God no!

CHARLOTTE. But he doesn't seem homosexual. He doesn't lisp.

BOB. Are you kidding?

CHARLOTTE. Well, he doesn't lisp, does he? Now what was I thinking of? Be quiet for a moment. (*Holds her head*) Secretary. The word I was looking for was secretary.

BOB. I mean didn't Bruce talk about us? Am I that unimportant to him?

CHARLOTTE. I really can't remember without access to the files. Let's talk about something else.

BOB. Something else?

CHARLOTTE. Oh, tell me about your childhood. At what age did you masturbate?

BOB. I don't want to talk about my childhood.

CHARLOTTE. Very well. We'll just sit in silence. New patients are difficult, aren't they, Snoopy? (*She nods Snoopy's head, glares at* BOB *significantly*)

BOB. May I see your accreditation, please?

(CHARLOTTE *starts to empty her drawer of junk again*)

BOB. (*Continued*) Never mind.

CHARLOTTE. So you and Bruce are an item, eh? Odd that I didn't pick that up.

BOB. Well we may be an item no longer.

CHARLOTTE. Well the path of true love never doth run smoothly.

BOB. I mean, suddenly there are all these women.

CHARLOTTE. Well if you're homosexual, I guess you don't find me attractive then, do you?

BOB. What?

CHARLOTTE. I guess you don't find me attractive, do you?

BOB. I don't see what that has to do with anything.

CHARLOTTE. Very well. We'll drop the subject. (*Pause*) Not even a teensy weensy bit? Well, no matter. (*Pause*) Tell me. What do you and Bruce do exactly?

BOB. What do you mean?

CHARLOTTE. You know what I mean. Physically.

BOB. I don't care to discuss it.

CHARLOTTE. Tell me.

BOB. Why do you want to know?

CHARLOTTE. Patients act out many of their deepest conflicts through the sexual act. Women who get on top may wish to feel dominant. Men who prefer oral sex with women may wish to return to the womb. Couples who prefer the missionary position may wish to do anthropological work in Ghana. Everything people do is a clue to a trained psychotherapist. (*Pause*) Tell me! Tell me!

BOB. I don't care to talk about it.

CHARLOTTE. Very well. We'll move on to something else. (*Sulks*) I'm sure I can guess what goes on anyway. (*Sulks*) I wasn't born yesterday. (*Pause; calmly*) Cocksucker.

BOB. What?

CHARLOTTE. Oh, I'm sorry. It was just this terrible urge I had. I'm terribly sorry. (*Gleefully*) COCK-SUCKER! (*Screams with laughter, rocks back and forth*) Oh my goodness, I'm sorry, I'm sorry. COCK-SUCKER! Whoops! Sorry. Oh God, it's my blood sugar. Help, I need a cookie. Help, a cookie! COCK-SUCKER! Wait, don't leave, I think I have a cookie in one of the drawers. Oh, I'm going to say it again, oh God! (*Screams the word as she stuffs cookie into her mouth, the word is muffled. Her body shakes with laughter and pleasure.*) Mmmm, cookie, cookie. Oh God. Oh God. (*Lies on floor, laughs slightly*) Oh, that was wonderful.

BOB. (*Stands, takes out a gun*) It's people like you who've oppressed gay people for centuries. (*Shoots her several times*)

CHARLOTTE. (*Startled; then:*) Good for you! Bravo! I like that. You're expressing your feelings, people have got to express their feelings. Am I bleeding? I can't find any blood.

BOB. It's a starting pistol. I bought it a couple of days ago, to threaten Bruce with.

CHARLOTTE. Good for you!

BOB. I don't want to go to prison. That's the only reason it's not a real gun.

CHARLOTTE. Good reason. You know what you want and what you don't want. Oh I like this directness, I feel I'm starting to help you. I mean, don't you see the similarity? Now why don't I have ulcers? Do you know?

(BOB *sits on floor next to her.*)

BOB. I don't know what you're talking about.

CHARLOTTE. I don't have ulcers because I don't repress things. I admit to all my feelings. Now a few minutes ago when I wanted to hurl anti-homosexual epithets at you, I didn't repress myself, I just let 'em rip. And that's why I'm happy. And when you were mad at me, you took out your toy gun and you shot me. And *that's* the beginning of mental health. I mean, do you understand what I'm saying?

BOB. Well I follow you.

CHARLOTTE. Oh we're making progress. Don't you see? And you said it yourself. You didn't buy the gun to shoot me, you bought it to shoot Bruce and that floozie of his. Right?

BOB. Yes.

CHARLOTTE. So you see what I'm getting at?

BOB. You mean, I should follow through on my impulse and go shoot Bruce and Prudence.

CHARLOTTE. (*Stands, staggers to her desk, overwhelmed with how well the session is going*) Oh I've never had such a productive first session!

BOB. (*Stands*) But should I get a real gun, or just use this one?

CHARLOTTE. That would be up to you. You have to ask yourself what you *really* want.

BOB. Well I don't want to go to jail, I just want to punish them.

CHARLOTTE. Good! Punish them! Act it out!

BOB. I mean, I could go to that restaurant right now.

CHARLOTTE. Oh yes! Oh good!

BOB. Will you come with me? I mean, in case someone tries to stop me you can explain it's part of my therapy.

CHARLOTTE. (*Agreeably*) Okay. Let me just get another cookie. Oh, I'm so glad you came to me. Now, should I bring Snoopy with me, or leave him here?

BOB. Well, which do you really *want*?

CHARLOTTE. Oh you're right. That's the issue, good for you. Okay, now...I don't know which I want. Let me sit here for a moment and figure it out. (SHE *sits and thinks, weighing pro-and-con-Snoopy ideas in her head; lights dim*)

ACT II

Scene 2

The restaurant again. BRUCE, PRUDENCE.

PRUDENCE. Why have we come back to this restaurant? We've been here twice before and never got any service.

BRUCE. You're upset about Bob, aren't you?

PRUDENCE. No. I understand. It's all difficult.

BRUCE. Bob will get used to the idea of us, I just tried to make it happen too soon. He's innately very flexible.

PRUDENCE. Then maybe the two of you should stay together.

BRUCE. Will you marry me?

PRUDENCE. Bruce, this is inappropriate.

BRUCE. Prudence, I believe one should just *act*—without thought, without reason, act on instinct. Look at the natives in Samoa, look at Margaret Mead. Did they think about what they were doing?

PRUDENCE. Important life decisions can't be made that way.

BRUCE. But they can, they must. Think of people who become heroes during emergencies and terrible disasters—they don't stop to fret and pick things apart, they just *move*, on sheer adrenalin. Why don't we think of our lives as some sort of uncontrollable disaster, like *The Towering Inferno* or *Tora! Tora! Tora!* and then why don't we just *act* on instinct and adrenalin. I mean, put that way, doesn't that make you just want to go out and get married?

PRUDENCE. But shouldn't I marry someone *specific*?

BRUCE. I'm specific.

PRUDENCE. Well, of course. But, what about the gas man? I mean, do I want the children saying I saw Daddy kissing the gas man?

BRUCE. We'd get electric heat.

PRUDENCE. Oh, Bruce!

BRUCE. Besides, I don't want lots and lots of people—I want you, and children, and occasionally Bob. Is that so bad?

PRUDENCE. Well it's not the traditional set-up.

BRUCE. Aren't you afraid of being lonely?

PRUDENCE. Well, I guess I am.

BRUCE. And aren't all your girlfriends from college married by now?

PRUDENCE. Well, many of them.

BRUCE. And you know you should really have children *now*, particularly if you may want more than one. I mean, soon you'll be at the end of your child-bearing years. I don't mean to be mean bringing that up, but it is a reality.

PRUDENCE. Can we talk about something else?

BRUCE. I mean time is running out for you. And me too. We're not twenty anymore. We're not even twenty-six anymore. Do you remember how old thirty used to seem?

PRUDENCE. Please don't go on, you're making me hysterical.

BRUCE. No, but these are realities, Prudence. I may be your last chance, maybe no one else will want to marry you until you're forty. And it's hard to meet people. You already said that Shaun Cassidy was too young. I mean, we have so little time left to ourselves, we've got to grab it before it's gone.

(STUART *enters, sees them, hides behind a table or large plant*)

PRUDENCE. Oh stop talking about time please. I mean, I know I'm thirty, it doesn't mean I'm dead.

BRUCE. I didn't say dead. I just said that our time on this earth is limited.

PRUDENCE. Stop talking, stop talking. (*Covers her ears*)

BRUCE. Prudence, I think you and I can make each

other happy. (*Sees* STUART) Do you see someone over there? Is that a waiter *hiding*?

PRUDENCE. (*Looks*) Oh for God's sake.

BRUCE. What is it?

PRUDENCE. It's my therapist.

BRUCE. Here?

PRUDENCE. I thought we were being followed. (*Calling*) Dr. Framingham, we see you.

BRUCE. What's he doing here?

(STUART *comes over to them*)

STUART. I want you to leave here with me this instant.

PRUDENCE. Why are you following me?

STUART. I'm going to give you a prescription for a sedative, and then I'm going to drive you home.

PRUDENCE. I can't believe that you've been following me.

STUART. I care about my patients. (*To* BRUCE) She's really *very* sick. The work we have to do together will take years.

PRUDENCE. Dr. Framingham, I've been meaning to call you since our last session. I'm discontinuing my therapy with you.

STUART. That would be very self-destructive. You'd be in Bellevue in a week.

PRUDENCE. I really don't want to see you ever again. Please go away now.

STUART. You don't mean what you say.

BRUCE. Do you want me to hit him?

PRUDENCE. No, I just want him to go away.

BRUCE. (*Stands*) The lady wants you to leave, mister.

STUART. (*To* PRUDENCE) So this is the degenerate you told me about?

BRUCE. What did she tell you about me?

PRUDENCE. Bruce, don't talk to him, please. Stuart, leave the restaurant. I'm tired of this.

STUART. Not until we set up our next appointment.

PRUDENCE. But, Stuart, I *told* you I'm discontinuing our therapy.

STUART. You haven't explained why to me.

PRUDENCE. Then I will. BECAUSE YOU ARE A PREMATURE EJACULATOR AND A LOUSY THERAPIST. NOW BEAT IT!

STUART. (*Very hurt, very mad*) Okay, Miss Sensuous Woman. But do you know what's going to happen to you without therapy? You're going to become a very pathetic, very lonely old maid. You know what's going to happen to you? You're going to break off with this clown in a few days, and then you're not going to go out with men anymore at all. Your emotional life is going to be tied up with your cats. (*To* BRUCE) Do you know what she does in her apartment? She keeps cats! Some guy she almost married last year wanted to marry her but he was allergic to cats and so *she* chose the cats!

PRUDENCE. That's not why we broke up at all!

STUART. You're gonna end up taking little boat cruises to Bermuda with your *cats* and with spinster librarians when you're fifty unless you decide to kill yourself before then! And all because you were too cowardly and self-destructive and stupid to keep yourself from being an old maid by sticking with your therapy!

PRUDENCE. You are talking utter gibberish. Michael was only *slightly* allergic to cats and we didn't get married because we decided we weren't really in love. And I'm not going to end up an old maid, I'm going to get married. In fact, I may even marry Bruce here. And if I do, Bruce and I will send you a picture of our children every Christmas to the mental institution where you'll be locked up!

STUART. (*Hysterical*) You're a terrible, terrible patient!

PRUDENCE. And you're a hideous doctor! I hate you!

(THEY *throw water at each other. Enter* BOB *and* MRS. WALLACE)

CHARLOTTE. Hello, everybody!

STUART. Who are these people?

CHARLOTTE. Go ahead, Bob, tell them.

BOB. I want to tell you how you've made me feel. I feel *very* angry. (HE *takes out his gun;* PRUDENCE, BRUCE *and* STUART *look terrified.* HE *fires the gun at them six or seven times.* THEY *are terribly shocked, stunned; are trying to figure out if* THEY'VE *been hit and are dying. Enter a young* WAITER)

WAITER. I'm sorry. We're going to have to ask you people to leave.

BRUCE. But we haven't even seen menus.

WAITER. I'm sorry. We can't have shootings in here.

STUART. Oh my God. Oh my God. (*Feels himself all*

over for wounds, just coming out of his fear)

PRUDENCE. (*Taking the gun from* BOB) Give me that. (*Points the gun at the* WAITER; WAITER *puts hands up*) Now look here, you. I am sick of the service in this restaurant. *I am very hungry.* Now I want you to bring me a steak, medium rare, no potato, two vegetables, a small salad with oil and vinegar and a glass of red wine. (*Angry, grouchy, waves gun toward the others*) Anyone else want to order?

CHARLOTTE. (*Raises hand*) I'd like to see a menu.

PRUDENCE. (*Waving the gun*) And bring these other people menus. And make it snappy.

WAITER. Yes, ma'am. (*Exits in a hurry*)

CHARLOTTE. (*To* PRUDENCE) Oh I *like* your direct-ness. Bravo!

STUART. (*Feeling for bullet holes*) I don't under-stand. Did he miss all of us?

PRUDENCE. Shut up and sit down. I'm going to eat some dinner, and I want everyone to shut up.

CHARLOTTE. Oh, I think she's marvelous.

PRUDENCE. (*Aims the gun at her*) Shut up.

CHARLOTTE. Sorry.

(EVERYONE *sits quietly.* WAITER *brings menus which* PEOPLE *look at except for* PRUDENCE, *who glares, and* STUART, *who's shaken*)

WAITER. Our specials today are chicken marsala cooked in a garlic and white wine sauce; roast Long Island duck with orange sauce . . .

(*Lights dim to black*)

ACT II

Scene 3

The restaurant still. THEY'*ve finished their dinners:*
PRUDENCE, BRUCE, BOB, MRS. WALLACE, STUART.
The WAITER *is clearing the dishes.*

CHARLOTTE. Mmmmm, that chocolate mousse was delicious. I really shouldn't have had two.

WAITER. (*To* PRUDENCE) Will there be anything else?

PRUDENCE. Just the check please.

(WAITER *exits*)

STUART. (*Who's still in a sort of shock; to* BOB) I thought you'd killed us all. You should be locked up.

BOB. Well, all's well that ends well.

CHARLOTTE. Please, I thought we'd exhausted the whole topic of the shooting. No harm was done.

STUART. What if I'd had a heart condition?

CHARLOTTE. That would have been your responsibility. We must all take responsibility for our own lives.

STUART. I think you're a terrible therapist.

CHARLOTTE. Sounds like professional jealousy to me.

PRUDENCE. (*To* STUART) I would not bring up the subject of who's a terrible therapist, if I were you.

CHARLOTTE. (*To* BRUCE) Oh, she's *so* direct, I just find her wonderful. Congratulations, Bruce.

PRUDENCE. What are you congratulating him on?

CHARLOTTE. Aren't you getting married?

BRUCE. Yes.   PRUDENCE. No.

(*Re-enter* WAITER)

WAITER. Here's the check. (MRS. WALLACE *calls for the check*) The second chocolate mousse was on the house, Mrs. Wallace.

CHARLOTTE. Thank you, honey. (*Kisses him on the cheek;* WAITER *exits*) He's one of my patients too.

BOB. He's quite attractive.

BRUCE. I thought you were going to kill yourself.

BOB. Mrs. Wallace helped me express my anger and now I don't feel like it anymore.

STUART. If one runs around shooting off guns, blank or otherwise, just because one is angry, then we'll have anarchy.

BOB. No one is interested in your opinion.

BRUCE. I think Prudence and I are a good match. I think we should get married as soon as possible.

PRUDENCE. I never want to get married, ever. I'm going to quit my job, and stay in my apartment until they evict me. Then I'm going to become a bag lady and live in the tunnels under Grand Central Station.

(THEY ALL *stare at her*)

BRUCE. (*To* PRUDENCE) If you marry me, I'll help you want to live again.

BOB. What am I supposed to do?

BRUCE. You seemed too busy with the waiter a minute ago.

BOB. For God's sake, I just looked at him. You're trying to go off and marry this woman. Really, you're just impossible. I thought after I shot at you, you'd get over this silly thing about women.

BRUCE. I need the stability of a woman.

BOB. You think she's stable? She just said she was going to become a bag woman.

BRUCE. She was speaking metaphorically.

BOB. What kind of metaphor is becoming a bag woman?

BRUCE. She meant she was depressed.

BOB. So I'm depressed too. Why don't you marry me? We'll go find some crackpot Episcopal minister somewhere, and then we'll adopt children together.

BRUCE. And that's another thing. I want to have my own children. I want to reproduce. She can give me children.

PRUDENCE. Please stop talking about me that way. I don't want to have your children. I want to be left alone. I want to become a lesbian and move in with Kate Millett.

BOB. Now she's making sense.

BRUCE. Don't make fun of her. She's upset.

BOB. I'm upset. No one worries about me.

BRUCE. Prudence, don't cry. We'll live in Connecticut. Everything will be fine.

STUART. Why doesn't she marry me? I make a good living. Prudence, as your therapist, I think you should marry me.

BRUCE. Prudence would never marry a man who didn't cry.

STUART. What?

BRUCE. You're too macho. Prudence doesn't want to marry you.

STUART. There's no such thing as macho. There's male and female, and then there's whatever you are.

(BRUCE *cries*)

STUART. (*Continued*) Oh, I'm sorry. Was it what I said?

CHARLOTTE. Bruce cries all the time. I encourage him to.

BRUCE. (*Having stopped crying; to* PRUDENCE) Why won't you marry me?

STUART. She should marry me.

PRUDENCE. No. I don't want to marry either of you. You're both crazy. I'm going to marry someone sane.

BOB. There's just me left.

PRUDENCE. No. I'll marry the waiter. Waiter!

CHARLOTTE. Oh dear, poor thing. Fear of intimacy leading to faulty reality testing. Prudence, dear, you don't know the waiter.

PRUDENCE. That doesn't matter. Bruce said it's better to know nothing about people when you get married.

BRUCE. But I meant you should marry me.

PRUDENCE. But I know too much about you and I know nothing about the waiter. Waiter!

(*Enter* WAITER)

WAITER. Is something the matter?

PRUDENCE. Yes. I want you to marry me.

WAITER. I don't understand. Did I add the check wrong?

PRUDENCE. No. I want you to marry me. I only have a few more years in which it's safe to have children.

WAITER. I don't understand.

CHARLOTTE. It's alright, Andrew. She's in therapy with me now.

PRUDENCE. (*Takes out the blank gun. Aims it at him*) Marry me! Marry me! (*Starts to giggle*) Marry me!

CHARLOTTE. It's alright, Prudence; you're my patient now. Everything's going to be alright.

PRUDENCE. I don't want any more therapy! I want tennis lessons!

CHARLOTTE. Now, dear, you're not ready for tennis yet. You must let me help you.

STUART. She's my patient.

CHARLOTTE. I think you've already failed her. I think I shall have to take her on.

PRUDENCE. (*Screams*) I don't want either of you! I've been to see several therapists and I'm sick of talking about myself!

(CHARLOTTE *throws a glass of water at* PRUDENCE)

CHARLOTTE. Enough of this self-destructive behavior, young woman!

(PRUDENCE, *furious, picks up another glass of water to throw back at Charlotte, hesitates momentarily, and throws it in* STUART'S *face.*)

CHARLOTTE. Bravo, good for you!

STUART. Why did she do that?

CHARLOTTE. She's getting in touch with her instincts. Prudence, you're making progress in my care already.

PRUDENCE. I HATE THIS RESTAURANT!

CHARLOTTE. The restaurant isn't the problem. You're looking for perfection. Prudence, you know the song "Someday My Prince Will Come"? Well, it's shit. There is no prince. Everyone in this world is limited; and depending on one's perspective is either horrible or "okay." Don't you agree, Dr. Framingham?

STUART. (*Just noticing*) I'm all wet.

CHARLOTTE. Ah, the beginnings of self-awareness, bravo, ruff ruff ruff! Oh that's right, I left Snoopy home. Well that was a wrong decision. Prudence, I'm making a point here. We're all alone, everyone's crazy and you have no choice but to be alone or to be with someone in what will be a highly imperfect and probably eventually unsatisfactory relationship.

PRUDENCE. I don't believe that's true.

CHARLOTTE. But you do. That's exactly why you act the way you do, because you believe that.

PRUDENCE. I believe there's more chance for happiness than that.

CHARLOTTE. You don't! And why should you? Look at Chekhov. Masha loves Konstantin, but Konstantin only loves Nina. Nina doesn't love Konstantin, but falls in love with Trigorin. Trigorin doesn't love Nina but sort of loves Madame Arkadina, who doesn't love anyone but herself. And Medviedenko loves Masha, but she only loves Konstantin, which is where we started out. And then at the end of the play, Konstantin kills himself. Don't you see?

PRUDENCE. What's your point?

CHARLOTTE. I've forgotten. Oh damn. Oh yes! My point is that everyone thinks Chekhov's plays are tragedies, but he called them comedies! It's all how you look at it. If you take psychological suffering in the right frame of mind, you can find the humor in it. And so that's how you should approach your relationship with Bruce.

BRUCE. This is getting too complicated.

PRUDENCE. My stomach feels queasy.

BRUCE. Never mind that. Prudence, remember what I said about acting on instinct, like you do in a crisis?

CHARLOTTE. (*Happily*) Like when I threw the water!

BRUCE. Right.

PRUDENCE. Yes I remember.

BRUCE. Okay. I want you to answer quickly now, on instinct, don't think about it, alright?

PRUDENCE. Alright.

BRUCE. Does your stomach feel queasy?

PRUDENCE. Yes.

BRUCE. Is your name Prudence?

PRUDENCE. Yes.

BRUCE. Is your dress wet?

PRUDENCE. Yes.

BRUCE. Will you marry me?

PRUDENCE. Yes.

(*There is a pause.*)

CHARLOTTE. Well, I'm glad that's settled.

STUART. You're not going to say yes like that, are you?

PRUDENCE. I guess so. All the other answers were yes. I have to go to the ladies room to throw up. Excuse me. (*Exits*)

BRUCE. I'm so happy. Not that she's sick, but that we're getting married.

BOB. (*Discontent*) Well, everyone's happy then.

STUART. All my patients leave their therapy. It's very upsetting.

CHARLOTTE. Would you like to talk about it?

BOB. (*To* ANDREW *the waiter*) Hi. I don't think we've actually met yet. My name is Bob.

ANDREW. Hi, I'm Andrew.

BOB. You look awfully familiar.

ANDREW. You've probably just seen my type.

BOB. Ah, well...

ANDREW. I get off in 5 minutes.

BOB. Need any help?

(*Everyone looks a bit aghast. Especially* BRUCE)

ANDREW. Could be. (*Exits*)

BRUCE. What are you doing?

BOB. Well if you expect me to live over the garage and let you carry on with that woman whenever you feel like it, then I'm allowed an occasional waiter.

STUART. Good God, he's not really going to live over the garage, is he?

CHARLOTTE. Well it depends on the zoning laws, I guess. (*Holds both sides of her head*) Uh, I'm getting a rush from all that mousse. Anyone feel like going to a disco?

BOB. I'm game. Bruce?

BRUCE. Not particularly. (*Nasty*) Maybe the waiter will want to go.

CHARLOTTE. Oh, Andrew is an excellent dancer! He's been to reform school.

BOB. Oh, he's sulking now.

BRUCE. I feel jealous about you and the waiter.

BOB. That's not very fair. What about you and Prudence?

BRUCE. You're right. But I still feel the emotion. And that's alright, isn't it, Mrs. Wallace?

CHARLOTTE. It's alright with me.

BRUCE. I feel happy about Prudence, and unhappy about the waiter. And I think I may want to cry. (*Tries*) No. False alarm.

(*Enter* ANDREW *in leather jacket*)

STUART. He certainly cries a lot.

CHARLOTTE. Don't you ever cry, Dr. Framingham?

STUART. Only when things fall on me.

CHARLOTTE. Oh yes! Do you all remember Skylab— that space thing that fell from the sky? That upset my porpoises very much.

STUART. You have porpoises?

CHARLOTTE. I'm sorry. Did I say porpoises? Andrew, what word do I want?

ANDREW. Patients.

CHARLOTTE. Yes, thank you. Patients.

ANDREW. We had this guy in reform school that we didn't like much. So we took this big heavy metal bird bath, and we dropped it on him. *He* didn't cry.

CHARLOTTE. That's interesting, Andrew.

ANDREW. He went into a coma.

CHARLOTTE. (*Stern*) Andrew, I've told you, I want you to have empathy for other people.

ANDREW. Oh right. I forgot. We felt real bad for him.

CHARLOTTE. Andrew has a real sensitivity in him; we just haven't seen any of it yet.

BOB. How long were you in reform school?

ANDREW. About 3 years. (*Grins*) Till it burned down.

BOB. Ah. (*Starting to think* ANDREW *may be a bad idea*) Great.

BRUCE. I hope Prudence isn't ill.

CHARLOTTE. Oh who cares? Let's go dancing!

BOB. Bruce, would you prefer I didn't go?

BRUCE. No, it's okay. I guess you're allowed waiters. We'll talk later. Have a nice time.

BOB. Thanks.

BRUCE. I think I better go check on Prudence. Good night, everybody. (*Gives* BOB *and* CHARLOTTE *hugs, exits*)

CHARLOTTE. He's so nice. Well, the music is calling all of us, I think.

ANDREW. (*To* BOB) My motorcycle's out this way.

BOB. My mother doesn't like me to ride motorcycles.

ANDREW. (*Shrugged off*) Fuck her.

STUART. (*To* CHARLOTTE) I don't think I want to go. I don't like discos.

CHARLOTTE. Nonsense. You must learn to like them.

STUART. There'll be too many women. I shouldn't tell you this, but I have troubles relating to women.

CHARLOTTE. Not to me. I think you're delightful.

STUART. You do?

CHARLOTTE. You know what I think? I think I could help you. I think you should come into therapy with me. I don't mean therapy, I mean thermidor.

ANDREW. No you mean therapy.

CHARLOTTE. Do I? It doesn't sound right. Thermidor. Thorazene. Thermometer.

BOB. No, he's right, you mean therapy.

CHARLOTTE. Therapy. Therapy? Thackery. Thespian. The second Mrs. Tanqueray. Ftatateeta. Finickulee, finickula. Well let's just go. It'll come to me. (*She starts to go; then*:) Ovaltine. Orca, the killer whale. Abba dabba dabba dabba dabba dabba dabba ...Oh, now I've really lost it.

(CHARLOTTE, STUART *and* ANDREW *exit. Enter* BRUCE *and* PRUDENCE)

PRUDENCE. Please, don't ever come into the ladies room after me again, alright? It's very disconcerting.

BRUCE. I was worried.

PRUDENCE. Where is everybody?

BRUCE. They went to a disco.

PRUDENCE. Why?

BRUCE. Something about the mousse Mrs. Wallace ate.

PRUDENCE. Never mind. I don't want to know.

BRUCE. Okay, now, answer on instinct again. Where in Connecticut do you think we should live? Quick, instinct!

PRUDENCF Bridgeport.

BRUCE. Oh, God, have you ever been to Bridgeport?

PRUDENCE. No, I meant Westport.

BRUCE. No, you said Bridgeport. There may be

some psychic reason it's right we live in Bridgeport.

PRUDENCE. No, please, we can't keep making decisions like this.

BRUCE. There are probably some lovely parts of Bridgeport.

PRUDENCE. Please, I don't want to live in Bridgeport. Bruce, why do you want to marry me. Answer on instinct.

BRUCE. I wrote it down earlier. (*He takes out typed piece of paper; reads:*) "I want to marry Prudence because all my life I keep fluctuating between being traditional and being insane. For instance, marrying Sally was my trying to be traditional; while sleeping with the gas man or that time I took my clothes off in the dentist's office were my going to the opposite extreme. But I'm not *happy* at either extreme. And that's where Prudence fits in. I feel she's very traditional, like Sally, but Sally has no imagination, she's too stable. And I think that even though Prudence is very traditional, she's very *un*stable and because of that I think we could be very happy together." Do you understand what I'm saying?

PRUDENCE. I don't understand what happened at the dentist's office.

BRUCE. Well, I needed root canal...

PRUDENCE. (*Getting upset*) And that wasn't on instinct. You'd written that down.

BRUCE. Well, I know. But it was an instinct to *read* it.

PRUDENCE. How can I marry someone who takes his clothes off at the dentist's office?

BRUCE. I don't take them off as a general rule. It just happened once.

PRUDENCE. (*Very upset*) I must be out of my mind.

BRUCE. Oh God, you're changing your mind, aren't you? Oh my God, oh my God. (*Sits down, weeps*)

(PRUDENCE *sits down, calm at first, then she too starts to cry. Then she starts to sob.* BRUCE *stops crying, looks up.*)

BRUCE. Prudence, you're crying. Don't cry. (*Holds her*) What's the matter?

PRUDENCE. (*Through weeping*) I don't know. I'm upset you took your clothes off at the dentist's office because that means you must be insane, and I thought maybe you weren't insane but just sort of, lively. (*Cries some more*)

BRUCE. I'm lively.

PRUDENCE. No, you're too lively. I wouldn't be able to cope.

BRUCE. (*Desperate to please her, keep her, comfort her*) Mrs. Wallace could give me lithium, she could give you speed. We might meet in the middle.

PRUDENCE. I don't want speed. I want an Alka-Seltzer. Do you think the waiter could get me one?

BRUCE. The waiter went to the disco with Bob.

PRUDENCE. Well there must be another waiter, don't you think?

BRUCE. Well it is a restaurant. (*Calls*) Oh waiter! Waiter! I don't see anybody.

PRUDENCE. I don't either. (*Calls*) Waiter!

BRUCE. I'm really honored you cried in front of me. Thank you.

PRUDENCE. You're welcome. Waiter!

BRUCE. I bet you don't cry very frequently.

PRUDENCE. No. Not in front of anyone at least.

BRUCE. I'm really honored.

PRUDENCE. I'll try to cry for you again sometime. Waiter!

BRUCE. Thank you. Waiter.

PRUDENCE. Waiter. Waiter.

BRUCE. Waiter. Waiter. This is a very existential restaurant.

PRUDENCE. (*A little woozy, a little sad, a little cheerful*) Yes, that's why I like it here so much.

BRUCE. You like it here?

PRUDENCE. Yes. Sort of. It's very comforting. They leave you alone here. It's conducive to conversation.

BRUCE. (*Very friendly, a basis for hope again*) Yes, it's a great place to talk.

PRUDENCE. (*Smiles, then futilely calls again*) Waiter. Waiter.

BRUCE. (*Makes a joke, sings:*) There's a waiter that I'm longing to see, duh duh duh duh...

BRUCE & PRUDENCE. (*Sing together, dreamily, a little rueful*) Duh duh duh duh, Dum dum dum dum, over me.

BRUCE. (*Smiles at her*) Silly song.

PRUDENCE. (*Smiles at him*) Very silly.

Curtain

AUTHOR'S NOTES

I have been sometimes delighted with the ease and talent with which some actors I've worked with have instinctively performed my plays just as I have envisioned them, or sometimes done them even better than I envisioned. And then, alas, I have sometimes been appalled by the way in which some actors (either on their own steam or confused by a wrong-headed director) have taken this same material and, by misinterpreting it or overstating it or misemphasizing it, have totally wrecked or changed the intention and tone of my plays. This latter group of actors is sometimes simply lacking in talent but, more frequently, they *are* talented people who are nonetheless lacking in the proper instinct for *my* plays; and sometimes they are laboring under the hateful (and frequently held) belief that comedy must be played "comically," with little winks (figurative or literal) at the audience and with no real emotion or real stakes in any of their playing. To quote an outside authority for a moment to back me up, here is the late Joe Orton writing production notes for the Royal Court's production of *Ruffian on the Stair*:

> ... The play is clearly not written naturalistically, but it must be directed and acted with absolute *realism*. No "stylization," no "camp." No attempt

in fact to match the author's extravagance of dialogue with extravagance of direction. REALISTIC
PLAYING AND DIRECTING.

Everyone of the characters must be real. None of
them is ever consciously funny. ... There must
never, from the actors, be the least hint of send-up.
The most ludicrous lines—those at the end of the
play for instance about the police and the goldfish
—must be played quite sincerely. Unless it's real
it won't be funny.[1]

I feel Orton's above advice regarding his play is true
of mine as well, and of most comedies. It is possible to
overdo taking the advice of playing the comedy for real
and to start playing it for *tragedy*—please don't do
that. Some instinctive balance is needed, but basically
his advice is good.

However, my purpose is not to complain about those
well-meaning souls who, lacking the right instincts or
just being pigheaded, muck things up. My purpose is
to try to give a sense of what acting and directing in-
terpretations I feel will enhance my plays, and specifi-
cally *Beyond Therapy*.

As of this date, the two favorite directors I have worked with have been Jerry Zaks and John Madden, both
of whom directed productions of *Beyond Therapy*.
(Zaks' other credits include the excellent off-Broadway premiere of my play *Sister Mary Ignatius Ex-*

[1]"Prick Up Your Ears; The Biography of Joe Orton," by
John Lahr, Published by Alfred A. Knopf, Inc. p. 130.

plains It All For You; and Madden's other credits include the excellent Broadway productions of Arthur
Kopit's *Wings* and Jules Feiffer's *Grown Ups.*) In any
case, I thought both Zaks and Madden did excellent
work on the two productions (Zaks off-Broadway, Madden on Broadway), and I'd like to explain some of the
planning and plotting that went into these two productions in the hopes they will assist others in putting on
this play.

Let's start with the casting. Bruce, for some reason, is
one of the hardest parts I've ever tried to cast. (If
Dudley Moore were a few years younger and were not
British, he would be perfect.)

For starters, Bruce claims he is bisexual; and it is
absolutely essential that he *truly* be that, absolutely
50-50. He should be attracted to women *and* to men;
he should *not* be a homosexual who is kidding himself
and trying to pretend to be heterosexual, that would be
unpleasing and malicious, and a lousy basis for a
comedy. He should truly find Prudence attractive, he
should truly want to be married with children in Connecticut, and he should truly find Bob and the gas man
attractive and emotionally appealing as well. As Bruce
says, "We have to accept contradictions in ourselves";
that is a wise statement on some level, yet in Bruce's
life his blithe acceptance of his duality is clearly creat-
ing chaos. He wants things to work out and with a kind
of blind optimism he just somehow believes that if he
keeps meaning well and trying to be nice to everyone
it will all work out. He's not very logical, but he's very
innocent. If ever he were to be knowing or calculating,
the play would change and be nasty. It's not meant to

be nasty, it's meant to be funny. Bruce's innocence and genuine 50-50 bisexuality are essential to its being funny.

Prudence is a bit easier to cast. Probably the major hurdle to overcome is to find that actress who can simultaneously be more than commonly intelligent (her quip "Perhaps not. But I can return to my apartment" is the remark of a witty woman), and yet be sufficiently uncertain of herself and vulnerable that she lets herself get into a stupid relationship with a macho-fool psychiatrist, and entertains a rather unlikely liason with Bruce because he touches certain buttons of hers ("I feel like I want to take care of you," he says in the first scene and she responds, suddenly, without judging her feelings or the inappropriateness of his offer, with "I would like that") and because on some level she eventually finds him fun (or "lively," as she says in the last scene).

Off-Broadway, Jerry Zaks and I cast Sigourney Weaver and Stephen Collins, who were charming and funny in the parts. Some critics complained that the pair were too good looking to need to put ads in the paper or to have trouble finding relationships. On the one hand, I think that's a stupid comment, as very good looking people have problems just like everybody else; and the critic who complained that it was unbelievable that beautiful Sigourney Weaver couldn't find a date for Saturday night was willfully missing the point—the point is Prudence can't find a *relationship* she likes, not a date.

However, that said, I must admit to some second feelings on this matter. It is true that Sigourney (a friend and a wonderful actress) is rather goddess-y beautiful, and that when you pair her with unusually handsome Steve Collins, maybe it is a trifle hard for us mere mortals to feel they're appropriate stand-ins for the rest of us floundering about. I also think, in retrospect, that Zaks and I perhaps erred in dressing Sigourney too traditionally and attractively; there is a real eccentricity in her appearance and talent that we could have made better use of. Still, the two gave lovely performances.

When it came time for the Broadway production over a year later, Sigourney was in Australia making a film, and the producer wished to have a brand new production with new director, mostly new cast, and new set. Regretfully missing the excellent Mr. Zaks (who, though, was busy mounting *Sister Mary Ignatius*, which as of this printing has run for over a year off-Broadway), I then had the good fortune to meet and work with John Madden on the play. For Bruce and Prudence, we cast John Lithgow and Dianne Wiest. Lithgow and Wiest, though indeed attractive, are not intimidatingly so as some critics complained of Weaver and Collins, so that issue was taken care of. Dealing with actors as talented as these four, I have no desire to compare them, because all were successful, excellent performances; but the different colors each brought can be suggestive of things to look for. Stephen Collins seemed sweetly comfortable with both sexes (I loved a moment Zaks gave him when he gave Bob a little hug before leaving him for a session with Mrs. Wallace) and rather controlled by his sex drive, both of which were excellent colors. Lithgow's mind seemed to have been scrambled so that he never knew quite why he did anything until *afterwards,* when he would do his best to explain it in retrospect (about telling Prudence he'd broken up with Bob when he hadn't: "Well, I lied. Sorry."), and this mental disarray was a wonderful color. Sigourney has a great gift in my stuff for saying things simply, as if what she is saying is as clear-cut and unforced as talking about the weather ("No it's nothing. It's just that I hate gay people.") and an ability to unleash real anger that still is funny (her extreme politeness in the face of Bob's scene 6 misbehavings finally exploding into her "Oh why don't you just go kill yourself!"); and both of these were invaluable colors for the character. And Dianne Wiest was a wizard on seeing when someone was crazy (her extreme discomfort saying "Thank you" when Bruce compliments her breasts after knowing her for two minutes) and then the next moment forgetting that judgment when a vulnerability is touched on (she seemed to melt into little girl sweetness on her "I would like that" when Bruce says he'd like to take care of her only a few seconds after his gaffe about her breasts). These few descriptions are just meant as indications of the kinds of things its good to look for and investigate in these two parts.

Before discussing the therapists, let me mention the part of Bob. From auditions and one reading, I've learned that there are two major things to avoid in the playing of Bob: avoid stereotyping (don't let him be bitchy gay, or effeminate) and avoid letting him play hostility to Prudence. Practically speaking, the audience will hate him if he's too mean to Prudence because the play is set up so that the audience has almost total sympathy with her. Also, let Bob be human and

smart enough to realize that *Bruce* has created this
awkward menage à trois, not Prudence, and that this
is rather typical and irritating behavior on Bruce's
part. Admittedly, in terms of the text, Bob acts very
immaturely around Prudence, but look for some of
the more sympathetic causes: he's afraid of losing
Bruce; he seems to be one of those gay activists who
believes everyone is gay, and so he finds Bruce and
Prudence baffling in their behavior. I don't want a
timid portrayal, and Bob is often angry and childish in
the extreme, but make sure he's not acting out of spite
towards Prudence (or, worse, toward women) but
out of fear that he's going to lose what he has with
Bruce. Bob is a baby, no question, just don't make him
a bitchy queen or a woman-hater. (Jack Gilpin did
very well with his sweet and befuddled portrayal in
both productions.)

As to the therapists, Stuart is clearly meant to be a
macho bully. On the other hand, he's also preposterous-
ly insecure, his ego deflated at any moment by some
woman's rejection of him. Thus, it's fairly tricky to
cast. If you cast someone who's too thoroughly in control and manipulative, the scenes he has with Prudence
can turn sinister and unfunny. On the other hand, the
actor, regardless of what he's like in real life, should
have a believable touch of the emotional-sexual fascist
that some women seem to get trapped by, or else the
humor when he bullies Prudence won't work. Further-
more, he should be *believably* sincere when he hands
Prudence his old "I can help you" line, and there should
be something appealing enough about him somewhere
that it is at least a little understandable how and why
Prudence slept with him twice. (Jim Borelli and Peter

Michael Goetz were two different and intriguing ways
to go with the part. Borelli, Italian as his name sug-
gests, seemed like a street kid grown-up who'd gone
to graduate school and medical school, but just never
left the attitudes of his high school buddies toward
masculinity and women behind him. Goetz, slightly
older and with a distinguished grey beard, seemed the
wise Freudian father figure who could easily take
Prudence in with his authoritative manner and yet had
just underneath that manner a galloping, raging in-
security that turned him alternately into a quivering
mess and a spiteful, shrieking bully.)

As for Mrs. Wallace, both productions featured Kate
McGregor-Stewart, who was hilarious and indelible in
the part. Kate had previously done wonderful "bitch
mothers" for me (notably in *Titanic* off-Broadway and
The Vietnamization of New Jersey at Yale Repertory
Theatre), and this was the first part I wrote that allowed her to be stark-raving mad *and* warm and loving
at the same time (as she is in life). For though Mrs.
Wallace is a loony, she's oddly "life-affirming." On
some level, her motivation really *is* to help her patients
have better lives and "express themselves," it's just
that I have her take things, often, to a foolish extreme.
She should not be played as a "ding bat," as I saw
in one production; she's crazy and her synapses, not
to mention her ability to remember words, are way,
way off. But when she makes sense, she makes sense.
(She truly believes in "to risk, to risk.") She is a
fond exaggeration.

Andrew the waiter is a small but fun part; and if
staged correctly, his entrance normally brings the

house down. Other than that, as the waiter dealing with customers he should be fairly polite; only as he gets chatty later do we need to see and hear some of his reform school quirks. (This interpretation—polite on the surface, but quirky-crazy on the inside—is how the two good actors Conan McCarty and David Pierce did the part in the two productions.) It is conceivable to play Andrew as more of a tough from the beginning; I saw it work more or less that way in another production; but it probably fits the world of the play better that Andrew seem like a normal, polite-cute waiter with problems underneath rather than a tough and maybe dangerous thug from the beginning.

Some miscellaneous thoughts and clarifications. Bruce's height as mentioned in the ad is obviously meant to reflect the height of the actor playing him. I wouldn't mention this except that someone once discussed the necessity of finding someone 6' to play Bruce; Stephen Collins and John Lithgow both happen to be 6', but certainly any height can play Bruce, just make sure that Mrs. Wallace's second ad in Scene 3 changes his height to make him taller than he is.

Also, because I once saw someone misinterpret it, when Mrs. Wallace barks for Snoopy as she does several times ("Good for you! Ruff ruff ruff!"), this is her eccentric manner of showing approval to her patients and offering them encouragement; as far as she's concerned, it's as normal, and as supportive, as saying "Good for you." She in no way thinks her stuffed dog is real. (The actress I saw misinterpreting it chose to play that the dog got excited and upset at certain times, and that *that's* what made the dog bark.

This struck me as quite unfunny and pushed Mrs. Wallace's eccentricity to the point where it was no longer remotely recognizable from life.)

In Scene 4 when Bruce cries, Prudence says "You're much too large to cry." This line was written with John Lithgow in mind since he is a very, very large man. If your Bruce is not large or is even small, please either cut the line or change it to "you and I are much too old to cry." With the "too old" comment, I feel she should include herself or it's a bit nasty.

In Scene 6 Prudence on her entrance into Bruce's apartment says, "It looks just like my apartment . . . And like my office at the magazine. And like the lobby at the bank. Everything looks alike." This line was used on Broadway (to good effect) and, of course, comments on the chic-modern taste of Bruce's furniture. The off-Broadway version had a different line I wanted to offer; the off-Broadway design utilized some of the same bits of furniture from scene to scene, so that Bruce's apartment included the big leather chair familiar from Prudence's therapist's office. Thus her line was then: ". . . And like my office at the magazine. And like my therapist's office. [SHE stares at the chair uncomfortably] Everything looks alike." The Broadway design, more elaborate than that for off-Broadway and making use of moving sets and a treadmill, did not use furniture from one scene overlapping to another, so the line no longer had point, and I changed it to the "lobby at the bank" line.

In Sence 6 (on p. 47) Prudence, desperately trying to make conversation with pharmacist Bob, asks "What exactly is in Tylenol, I wonder?" How times change.

This was obviously written before the maniac in Chicago started putting cyanide in Tylenol tablets. Clearly the reference no longer works, though I thought I'd leave it in the printed text for posterity. The original joke obviously has to do with referring to some common pharmaceutical drug that we all use but have little sense of what's in it; I can't decide on the exactly right replacement, but "Dexatrim" or "Gelusil" would probably do.

In Scene 6, Bob's mother Sadie calls on the phone frequently, and I wanted to pass on a funny device that Jerry Zaks came up with off-Broadway. Somehow the phone, whose rings were nonetheless still controlled by the stage manger, was hooked up as a real phone to backstage, and we had a real actress (in this case, Kate McGregor-Stewart, our Mrs. Wallace) actually on the phone as Sadie. Basically we never heard any dialogue she said (nor should we), but at those times when Sadie was singing, the audience could make out the faint sound of some crackpot woman singing over the telephone, and it was very funny. (In the larger house on Broadway, the effect would've been lost, and so we dispensed with it.)

At the opening of Act II, Bruce says "... we're going to be at the Restaurant. I mean that's the name of the restaurant." I have never been able to comfortably name this restaurant; off-Broadway we called it the Squire Restaurant. I changed it to The Restaurant because the Broadway set had a delicate neon sign upstage that said, generically I guess, Restaurant; and I didn't want to confuse the audience with a name they hadn't head; I wanted them to know (or presume) that

Bruce was going to the same restaurant as Scenes I and 4 of Act I. So in any case, please feel free to choose another name for the restaurant, as long as it sounds moderately expensive and a place young singles would hang out in. I also don't think it should be a foreign restaurant.

On page 73 Mrs. Wallace says that everyone is either "horrible or 'okay.' " Again, since I once saw it misinterpreted, by "okay" Mrs. Wallace means, rather depressingly, "just so-so"; she does not mean "okay" in the sense of "everything's fine."

A couple of words about the ending (especially pages 80 and 81). When Bruce and Prudence call "Waiter" all those times, I don't mean for them to be bellowing or getting angry, or to get any comic mileage from their talking softly one minute and then yelling "waiter" the next. Since they (and the audience) have spent a great deal of time in this restaurant without ever getting service (except from Andrew at gunpoint), Bruce and Prudence, though hoping a little they might possibly find another waiter, nonetheless are smart enough to know that it's only a chance, far from a certainty; plus they are both so emotionally exhausted and confused, that their focus really does remain themselves and their own unhappiness/disappointment. Particularly by the last cluster of "Waiter"'s, they call wistfully, and it really *is* a meaningless, existential gesture; Bruce's comment to that effect is an accurate one.

As to the ending itself, Prudence really has realized that marrying Bruce is probably not something that will work out; yet it is true that, through all the hysteria, Bruce and Prudence do enjoy one another's company and if their relationship is a "miss," it's a near-miss. So when Bruce makes his joke singing "There's a waiter that I'm longing to see," there is a friendly, after-the-crying feel between the two of them; as they get into singing (softly) the pretty melody of the song they both get a little spacey, a little melancholy. The final direction that they smile at each other (as they say "Silly song"; "Very silly") is not meant as any big upbeat ending; the ending is, to choose a word, rueful. Since the play is a comedy and not some tragicomedy about failed relationships, it might seem heavy-handed and depressing if Bruce and Prudence didn't look at one another at the end with some amount of fondness. I'm sure it will vary from actor to actor. If having the actors smile at one another makes it seem that they will get married for certain, then don't do it. The ending to aim for is one of ambiguity: they're sorry they can't seem to find exactly what they want in each other, they're rueful if they're about to finally break it off, they're hopeful since it *is* true through it all they like one another. You take it from there I guess.

What other things to say? The physical world of the play is chic and modern, lots of hanging plants and modern furniture with sleek lines. Both of the excellent designers, Karen Schultz and Andrew Jackness, set the play in a very real world with real furniture, Ms. Schultz using Museum of Modern Art-ish bright primary colors, and Mr. Jackness using more muted colors and recessed lighting sorts of effects, and with scene changes that seemed inexplicably witty, with the main set coming in on a wagon from one side, while the bulk of the furniture rode in on a treadmill from the other side.

I would imagine other sets would be less elaborate than the Broadway one. One major thing to watch out for is the amount of time it takes to go from scene to scene. There is a real value in being able to change scene with no pause in between; probably, though, the only way to accomplish that totally would be to use a non-realistic set (you know, with big building blocks for furniture; that sort of thing); if designed attractively and cleverly, that sort of set would probably be fine, though then be sure the costumes and acting keep rooting the play back to recognizable reality, it's not a cartoon.

And about the advice I started this essay with, about playing the comedy for real, please, please, please don't take it so seriously that you turn the play into a soap opera or some awful non-funny docu-drama about young singles. The opening advice, from me and Mr. Orton, is to go for that kind of comedy that is based in character and real feelings—to give movie examples, for instance, go for the "real" comic acting of Diane Keaton, say, in *Annie Hall,* not for the broad, cartoony acting used in the various Mel Brooks movies, however funny and appropriate that style may be to his films.

That's all. Stay well, keep in touch, good luck with the production. Please don't change my lines willy-nilly, it makes me cry. It you were a writer, you'd be a writer. And if you are a writer, then change your own lines, not mine.

Christopher Durang
New York City
December, 1982

BRUCE

I-1

Navy blazer
Blue shirt
Gold neck chain (no tie)
Grey slacks
Grey socks
Loafers
Watch

I-3

Blue shirt
Blue boat neck sweater
Olive corduroy slacks
Olive socks
Suede shoes

I-4

Take off sweater
Add tie
Corduroy jacket (matches slacks)

I-6

Pink shirt
Burgundy tie

3/4 length chef's apron
Olive socks
Suede shoes

II-1
Blue shirt
Olive corduroy suit
Olive socks
Tie
Suede shoes

PRUDENCE
I-1
Magenta knit dress
String of pearls
Tan open-toed sling backs
Shoulder bag

I-2
Burgundy straight skirt
Vertical striped blouse (purple tones)
Shoes
String of pearls
Blue glasses
Shoulder bag

I-4
Blue side buttoned straight skirt
Red and blue striped blouse
Blue round earrings
Navy pumps
Scarf

I-5

    Grey straight skirt
    High collar ruffled blouse
    Grey jacket
    Beige pumps
    Shoulder bag

I-6

    Pink silk blouse
    Mauve knit skirt
    Elastic belt
    Dark shoes
    Pink and blue woven shawl

II

    Repeat I-6 clothes

CHARLOTTE

I-3

    Purple skirt
    Turquoise blouse
    Purple vest
    Squash blossom neckless
    Turquoise and pink wedgies
    Watch

II-1

    Purple velvet caftan
    Blue and red and purple shawl
    Low purple canvass espadrilles
    Shoulder bag
    Bracelets

STUART

  I-2
- Tweed suit
- Grey shoes
- Grey socks
- Watch
- Rings

  I-5
- Dark sport coat
- Blue shirt
- Grey slacks
- Grey socks
- Loafers
- Watch
- Rings

  II-2
- Navy blazer
- Purple shirt
- Blue jeans
- Dark socks
- Dark loafers
- Watch
- Rings

BOB

  I-6
- Blue jeans
- Solid brick red rugby shirt
- White sweat socks
- No shoes

II

    Add blue down quilted vest
    Blue running shoes

ANDREW

  II-2

    Black pants
    Black socks
    Black running sheos
    Black tie
    White shirt
    Black waiters apron

  II-3

    Add black leather motorcycle jacket
    Black leather gloves
    Silver motorcycle helmut

PROPS

RESTAURANT
  Table, center
    2 chairs
    Table cloth
    2 silver set ups
    2 napkins
    2 glasses w/1" of warm water in each
    Salt and pepper shakers
    1 vase w/cloth flowers
  1 potted plant stage right
  1 potted plant stage left
  Table left
    2 chairs
    2 silver set ups
  2 glasses (empty)
    2 napkins
    1 vase w/cloth flowers
  Right table
    2 chairs
    2 silver set ups
    2 glasses (empty)
    2 napkins
    1 vase w/cloth flowers

  Lamp on center of each table

101

STUART'S OFFICE

Small table up left
- Water pitcher
- Date book
- Lamp

Desk (Drawers not practical)
- cigarette holder
- Merit cigarettes
- Telephone
- Intercom
- Address book
- Ash tray
- Lighter—fancy desk kind
- Bic hand lighter
- Assorted pens/pencils
- Chair left of desk (no arms)

Book shelf stage right
- Clipboard w/paper, fancy pen
- Stuart's glasses
- Stuart's pipe

Waste can above desk

Blinds on window half open

Psychiatrist couch

Arm chair

Small side table
- Box of kleenex
- Ash tray

Desk chair

CHARLOTTE'S OFFICE

Small table above door
- Lamp

Low blue sofa
- Assorted throw pillows

Child's drawings on walls
Child's drawing in cabinet under book shelf
Plant watering can on book shelf
Scoop chair w/arms
Scoop chair (armless)
White swivel chair w/casters
White waste basket
Desk (one large practical drawer)
    Boutique tissue
    Intercom phone
    Pink appointment book
    Steno pad open to blank page
    2 sharp pencils
    Cup of water
In large desk drawer:
    Bundle of rope
    Binnoculars
    Empty orange juice container
    6 old fashioned pocket file folders w/assorted
      papers
    Clip board with old newspaper clippings, loose
      papers · very messy looking
Coffee table
2 arm chairs (match the sofa)

BRUCE'S APARTMENT
Sofa
Sofa table
    Phone
    Plant
    Small address book
End table
    Lamp
    Ash tray

2 book cases
Lamps

PROP TABLE RIGHT
2 copies of "The New York Review of Books"
2 glasses of sparkling water with plastic ice cubes
2 plants
1 copy of People magazine
Starting pistol-loaded
Back-up starting pistol for stage manager to
    cover shots with
4 menu's
Dinner check on small tray
Waiter's pad and pencil
Typed letter (Text on page 2-3-30)

PROP TABLE STAGE LEFT
Bob's suit case
Crash box
Bottle of wine in brown paper bag
Glass of red wine

PERSONAL PROPS
CHARLOTTE:
    Snoopy
    Perfume in spray bottle
    Play money
STUART:
    Bic lighter
    Cigarette case
    Watch

PROP MOVES

ACT I

Scene 1. The Restaurant
  On Center Wagon:
    Table (left)
    2 chairs
    Table set up:
      Table cloth, 2 cloth napkins, 1 knife, 2 forks,
      2 spoons, Salt and Pepper shakers, Small vase
      with Cloth Flowers, Small Electric Lamp with
      Small shade.
    Table (right)
    2 chairs
    Table set up
  On Treadmill:
    Table (center)
    2 chairs
    Table set up
    Potted plant (left)
    Potted plant (right)
SET CHANGE:
  Stage left Treadmill *Strike*;:
    Table
    2 chairs
    2 potted plants
  Stage Right Treadmill *Load*:

Arm chair
Stage Right Treadmill *Load*:
Arm chair
Psychiatrist couch
Small side table w leenex box
Ash tray
Large desk chair

Scene 2. Dr. Stuart Framingham's Office
On Left Wagon:
Desk
Side chair
Small table w/water pitcher
SET CHANGE:
Stage Left Treadmill *Load*:
Scoop chair w/arms
Desk
White swivel chair w/casters
White waste basket
Scoop chair (armless)
Stage right Treadmill *Strike*:
Arm chair
Psychiatrist couch
Small side table
Large desk chair

Scene 3: The Office of Charlotte Wallace
On Right Wagon:
Small potted plant
Small sofa w/throw pillows
SET CHANGE:
Stage Left Treadmill *Strike*:
Scoop chair w ms

Desk
White swivel chair w/casters
White waste basket
Scoop chair (armless)
Stage Right Treadmill *Load*:
Restaurant table
2 chairs
Table set up
2 potted plants

Scene 4: The Restaurant Again
  On Center Wagon: 9 (Same as Scene 1.)
SET CHANGE:
  Stage Left Treadmill *Strike*:
    Restaurant table
    2 chairs
    Table set up
    2 potted plants
  Stage Right Treadmill *Load*:
    Arm chair
    Psychiatrist couch
    Small side table
    w/Kleenex
      Ash tray
    Large desk chair

Scene 5: Dr. Framingham's Office
  On Center Wagon: (Same as Scene 2)
  Note: Change Up Stage Center Wagon from Restaurant to Living Room.
SET CHANGE:
  Stage Left Treadmill *Load*:
    Coffee table

2 arm chairs (match sofa)
Stage right Treadmill *Strike*:
    Arm chair
    Psychiatrist couch
    Small side table
    Desk chair

Scene 6: Bruce's Apartment
  On Center Wagon:
    Large sofa
    End table
    Sofa table
    w/plant
      Telephone
      Address book
    Side table
    w/small lamp
    2 book cases
    w/books
    Lamps
    Plants

INTERMISSION
  Note: Change Center Wagon from Bruce's Apart-
  ment back to The Restaurant.
  PRE-SET:
    Mrs. Wallace's Office

ACT II

Scene 1: Mrs. Wallace's Office
SET CHANGE:
  Stage Left Treadmill *Load*:

Restaurant table
3 chairs
Table set up
2 potted plants
Stage Right Treadmill *Strike*:
Scoop chair w/arms
Desk
White swivel chair w/casters
White waste basket
Scoop chair (armless)

Scene 2: The Restaurant Again
On Center Wagon:
(Same as Scene 1. Act I)
SET CHANGE:
Stage Left Treadmill *Load*:
3 restaurant tables
2 chairs
Table set ups
Assorted dirty dishes
1 potted palm
Stage Right Treadmill Strike:
Restaurant table
Table set up
2 chairs
1 potted palm

Scene 3: The Restaurant Still
On Center Wagon:
(Same as ACT II, Scene 2.)

SET CHANGE:
  Stage Left Treadmill *Strike*:
    3 Restaurants
    2 chairs
    Assorted dirty dishes
    2 potted plants

  BOWS
    (Treadmill moves only with actors on it)

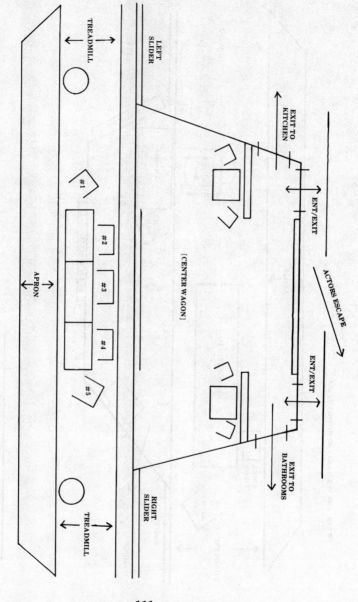

THE RESTAURANT — Act II - Sc 3

LEFT SLIDER

TREADMILL

EXIT TO KITCHEN

ENT/EXIT

ACTORS ESCAPE

#1

[CENTER WAGON]

#2

#3

#4

#5

APRON

ENT/EXIT

EXIT TO BATHROOMS

RIGHT SLIDER

TREADMILL

111

DR. FRAMINGHAM'S OFFICE — Act 1 · Sc 2 & 5

TREADMILL

SLIDER

LEFT

BOOKCASE

DESK

DESK CHAIR

SIDE CHAIR

NYC — WINDOW SCENE

APRON

PSYCHIATRIST COUCH

SMALL TABLE

ARM CHAIR

ENT/EXIT

SLIDER

TREADMILL

RIGHT

STAGE LEFT WAGON

112

TREADMILL

LEFT SLIDER

TO KITCHEN

CHAIR

PLANT

LIGHT

BOOKCASE

NYC — WINDOW SCENE

BOOKCASE

TABLE

PLANT PHONE ADDRESS BOOK

SOFA

PEOPLE

APRON

COFFEE TABLE

TABLE

CHAIR

TO HALL AND BEDROOMS

TREADMILL

RIGHT SLIDER

BRUCE'S APARTMENT — Act I · Sc 6

113

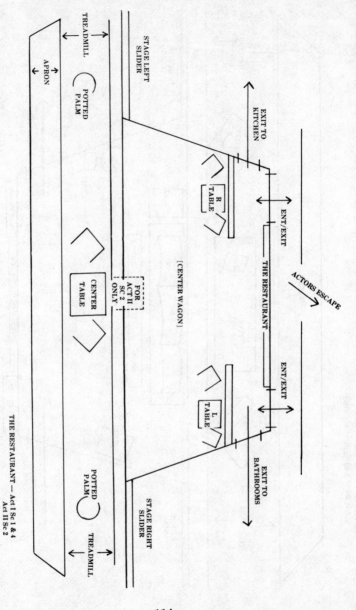

THE RESTAURANT — Act I Sc 1 & 4
Act II Sc 2

114

TREADMILL.

LEFT
SLIDER

ENT/EXIT

PLANT

TABLE

SCOOP
CHAIR
W/ARMS

APRON

WHITE
WASTE
BASKET

SWIVEL
CHAIR

DESK

NYC — WINDOW SCENE

SMALL SOFA

BOOKCASE

CABINET
UNDER

ARMLESS
SCOOP
CHAIR

RIGHT
SLIDER

TREADMILL.

STAGE RIGHT WAGON

CHARLOTTE WALLACE'S OFFICE
Act I — Sc 3
Act II — Sc 1

115

Other Publications for Your Interest

COMING ATTRACTIONS
(ADVANCED GROUPS—COMEDY WITH MUSIC)

By TED TALLY, music by JACK FELDMAN, lyrics by BRUCE SUSSMAN and FELDMAN

5 men, 2 women—Unit Set

Lonnie Wayne Burke has the requisite viciousness to be a media celebrity—but he lacks vision. When we meet him, he is holding only four people hostage in a laundromat. There aren't any cops much less reporters around, because they're across town where some guy is holding 50 hostages. But, a talent agent named Manny sees possibilities in Lonnie Wayne. He devises a criminal persona for him by dressing him in a skeleton costume and sending him door-to-door, murdering people as "The Hallowe'en Killer". He is captured, and becomes an instant celebrity, performing on TV shows. When his fame starts to wane, he crashes the Miss America Pageant disguised as Miss Wyoming to kill Miss America on camera. However, he falls in love with her, and this eventually leads to his downfall. Lonnie ends up in the electric chair, and is fried "live" on prime-time TV as part of a jazzy production number! "Fizzles with pixilated laughter."—Time. "I don't often burst into gales of laughter in the theatre; here, I found myself rocking with guffaws."—New York Mag. "Vastly entertaining."—Newark Star-Ledger.

(Royalty, $50-$40.)

SORROWS OF STEPHEN
(ADVANCED GROUPS—COMEDY)

By PETER PARNELL

4 men, 5 women—Unit set

Stephen Hurt is a headstrong, impetuous young man—an irrepressible romantic—he's unable not to be in love. One of his models is Goethe's tragic hero, Werther, but as a contemporary New Yorker, he's adaptable. The end of an apparently undying love is followed by the birth of a grand new passion. And as he believes there's a literary precedent for all romantic possibilities justifying his choices—so with enthusiasm bordering on fickleness, he turns from Tolstoy, to Stendhal or Balzac. And Stephen's never discouraged—he can withstand rivers of rejection. (From the N.Y. Times.) And so his affairs—real and tentative—begin when his girl friend leaves him. He makes a romantic stab at a female cab driver, passes an assignation note to an unknown lady at the opera, flirts with an accessible waitress—and then has a tragic-with-comic-overtones, wild affair with his best friend's fiancée. "Breezy and buoyant. A real romantic comedy, sophisticated and sentimental, with an ageless attitude toward the power of positive love."—N.Y. Times.

(Slightly Restricted. Royalty, $50-$40, where available)

Other Publications for Your Interest

PAST TENSE
(LITTLE THEATRE—DRAMA)
By JACK ZEMAN

1 man, 1 woman, 2 optional men—Interior

This compelling new play is about the breakup of a marriage. It is set on the day Emily and Ralphy Michaelson, a prosperous middle-aged couple, break off a union of 27 years. As they confront each other in their packed-up living room one final time, they alternately taunt and caress one another. She has never forgiven him for a petty infidelity of years ago. He has never forgiven her for her inability to express grief over the long-ago accidental death of their youngest child. In a series of flashbacks, Mr. Zeman dredges up the pivotal events of their characters' lives. Barbara Feldon and Laurence Luckinbill starred on Broadway in this at times humorous, and ultimately very moving play by a talented new playwright. " . . . rich in theatrical devices, sassy talk and promising themes."—N.Y. Times. "There is no doubt that Zeman can write. His backbiting, backlashing dialogue has considerable gusto—it belts out with a most impressively muscular vigor and intellectual vivacity."—N.Y. Post.

(Royalty, $50-$35)

SCENES AND REVELATIONS
(ALL GROUPS—DRAMA)
By ELAN GARONZIK

3 men, 4 women—Platform set

Set in 1894 at the height of America's westward movement, the play portrays the lives of four Pennsylvania sisters who decide not to move west, but to England. It opens with the sisters prepared to leave their farm and birthplace forever. Then a series of lyrical flashbacks dramatize the tender and frustrating romances of the women. Rebecca, the youngest, marries and moves west to Nebraska, only to find she is ill-prepared for pioneer life. Millie, a bohemian artist, falls in love with the farm boy next door; when he marries a woman without Millie's worldly aspirations, she is crushed. Charlotte, a nurse, is rejected by her doctor on religious principles. Only Helena, the eldest, has the promise of a bright and bold life in California with Samuel, the farm's manager. However, Rebecca's tragic return east moves the sisters to unite for the promise of a better life in England. "A deeply human play . . . a rocket to the moon of imagination," Claudia Cassidy—WFMT, Chicago. "Humanly full . . . glimmers with revelation," Elliott—Chicago Sun-Times. "The play is a beauty," Sharp—WWD. "A deep understanding of women and their relationships with men," Barnes—New York Post.

(Royalty, $50-$35.)